Out of the Storm

GLORIA BOSTIC

Live victoriously!
Gloria Bostic

Copyright © 2016 Gloria Baer Bostic
All Rights Reserved

This is a work of fiction. Names, characters, businesses, places, events and incidents are either the products of the author's imagination or used in a fictitious manner. Any resemblance to actual persons, living or dead, or actual events is purely coincidental.

Year of the Book
135 Glen Avenue
Glen Rock, Pennsylvania

ISBN 13: 978-1-942430-58-2
ISBN 10: 1-942430-58-2

Library of Congress Control Number: 2016935700

This book is dedicated

To all the children who are living in a prison of secrets:
Though it may seem hopeless, speak out, find help – Know you are loved.

To the young women burdened with memories of a lost childhood:
You are not alone. You are loved.

To the women who have survived against
insurmountable odds and thrown off the mantle of victim:
You are a survivor!

You are victorious!

I also dedicate this to all those who extend their hands to
help victims of abuse find their way from the darkness of depression
into the light of a life filled with possibilities.

Acknowledgments

I want to thank my husband, Lee, for always being there and never letting me take myself or my work too seriously, yet never doubting that I will accomplish all that I set out to do. I love doing life with you.

I want to thank my sons, Mike, John, and Eddie Baer for bringing joy into my life by their very being. You gave my life meaning and purpose and taught me the real meaning of love. You have my heart.

I want to thank my grandchildren, Mike Jr., Elise, Emily, and Grace for multiplying the love in my life beyond my imaginings.

I want to thank my sister and friend, Darleen Muhly, who is always there to love and support me.

I also want to thank my writing group for their constant encouragement, love, and support. Your friendship has enriched my life.

Finally, I want to thank Demi Stevens who saw the possibilities in me and in a manuscript that had been in a drawer for five years. It is only because of your vision, your dedication, and your encouragement and support throughout this whole process that I was able to accomplish this. I appreciate you!

Chapter 1

June 2000

Greta stared at her reflection in the mirror. Wrapped in her own arms, it was the closest thing to a hug she would have on her fifteenth birthday. Sure, there would be cake and candles, and she would blow them out, and then watch as her wish went up in smoke. It was a simple wish, but like every other year, she knew it was foolish to believe it would ever come true.

"Happy birthday to me," she whispered.

Her light brown hair with golden highlights flowed softly, framing her fair skin and blue eyes. She recognized her German ancestry and knew boys were attracted at first glance. Sad eyes returned the stare until she turned away, remembering how Jimmy had smiled and waved after school yesterday... and how she'd pretended not to see him.

Since fifth grade, boys had been vying for her attention. Greta was flattered but knew better than to respond. All through middle school those same boys had teased and pursued her. Sometimes she wondered what it would be like to hang out with them, just to be normal. But now in high school, when Jimmy really did ask her out, she'd pushed him away.

Maybe someday... but not now... unless...

Greta picked up her sketchpad and pencil, sat at her desk, and began drawing. This was her escape, her art, her dream. It was only a temporary one though, as reality crept back into her mind. She wondered what Jimmy must think of her and decided to give it one more try at dinner.

"No! You're a fourteen-year-old child. Absolutely not." Uncle Don didn't even look up from his plate as he loaded his fork with another chunk of meat.

"I'm fifteen... and it's... " Greta began, but was cut off.

"Since when?" he asked, then grunted when his wife whispered, "It's her birthday."

Taylor shot her a warning glance. "Oh, yeah, well you're *still* a child, and the answer is still no," he finished emphatically.

Not so much as a Happy Birthday, Greta thought pushing the food around her plate. She screwed up her courage to try again. "But, it's not really a date. I mean, it's a group of us that..." The look on her uncle's face choked out the rest of her sentence. Silence.

"Don," Kim Taylor said softly, "maybe since it's her birthday..."

"I said no!" he bellowed. "And if I want your opinion I'll ask for it."

Since going to live with them after her father and grandmother's tragic deaths, Greta had learned her aunt seldom dared to express disagreement with her uncle.

Not another word was uttered. Greta saw her aunt's look of pity and knew it was hopeless. The rest of the meal dragged on in uncomfortable silence.

As Greta brooded, she remembered that her cousin Bobby had been just fifteen when Greta had moved in. "Bobby dated when he was fifteen," she said meekly.

Five years older than her, Uncle Don and Aunt Kim's son Bobby was away at college now. But Greta could remember how he had often stayed out late that first year she'd moved in with them.

"You're a girl. It's different for girls," her Uncle Don said. "You know what all boys want from you." He glanced her way and Greta looked back down at her plate. "And I'm going to see they don't get it!"

Greta knew. Yes, of course she knew. Uncle Don had taught her all about that subject.

Chapter 2

Spring 2004

Greta was in love...

She met Tony on a blind date, discreetly wiping her sweaty palms on her skirt before accepting his warm handshake. The heat jumped from his touch, warming her to the core.

That was just the beginning of a flame that would nearly consume them both. Her friend Maria, who'd set them up, had done well.

"So you're an only child?" he asked. "I can't even imagine what that's like. I have three brothers and two sisters." Tony leaned back in his chair and laughed. "I bet your dinner table was a lot quieter than what goes on in our house."

Greta couldn't take her eyes off that smile.

"Yes, it was pretty quiet. My Dad didn't talk much... but when I was little, I kind of made up for it. I was quite the chatter-box back then." Greta looked up from her plate and grinned. Tony's eyes crinkled when he returned her smile.

"You should hear my sisters," he laughed. "Talk about chatter-boxes."

Greta listened as he talked about his family, but her attention was on more than his words. Tony's thick, dark hair bespoke his Italian heritage. He wore it combed straight back with just that one wild, wavy lock that insisted on tumbling to the side, tickling his temple. Greta's hand itched to reach up and brush it back, a practice that would become habit over time.

By the time their waiter placed lemon meringue pie in front of her, Greta was already hungry for a much sweeter dessert.

※

In the months that followed, Greta lost herself completely in this new love. She and Tony saw each other nearly every day, and the heat between them was stoked each time. Greta was already imagining their happily ever after—living in a three-bedroom home with their two beautiful children, a boy and a girl, and perhaps even a collie puppy.

But consumed as she was, she couldn't escape that nagging fear. *Why am I always waiting for something to go wrong?*

It wasn't long before they reached the point that had scared her. When she was with Tony, Greta felt like she was melting into him. When they kissed, she wanted more.

"I love you, Greta," he whispered, and she felt his breath on her neck. Yes, she wanted more. She felt his hand on her thigh. His touch set her on fire. This time she wouldn't stop him. Her trembling hand touched his cheek.

"I love you, Tony."

When he touched her, she couldn't get enough... she wanted him, and yet, when the moment came for that final intimacy, her body tensed for the pain she knew would follow. This would be her first time with a man—at least by choice—but she knew what was coming.

"What is it, Greta? Am I hurting you?"

"No," she reassured, pulling him close and urging him on, knowing it would soon be over. Only then could she relax in his arms and feel completely safe and loved once again.

A few moments of pain is a small price to pay for a love like ours, Greta rationalized. She wanted to spend every waking moment with Tony. Blinded by love, Greta was sure this was real, and that they would live happily ever after.

She was wrong.

⁂

"Yes! You finally got the call right, ref! About damn time!"

Greta laughed hearing Tony yell at the TV. He was passionate about his sports teams. He was passionate about everything. She grabbed a cold beer from the frig, picked up the glass of iced tea she'd just poured herself, and carried them into the living room.

"Here you go. I figured you might be ready for another beer." Greta put the bottle on a coaster on the side table and started to sit on his lap.

"What are you doing? You're going to spill that all over us!"

Greta jumped back up. *It wouldn't have spilled if you hadn't scared me like that,* she thought. Grabbing another coaster, she started to put it down on the table next to Tony's.

"Why don't you just sit on the sofa where there's more room?" Tony said dismissively.

Greta looked at an unfamiliar face, not understanding his knitted brow or the clenched fists in his lap. Tony's body turned into itself as he stared at the TV. There were no open arms. He pushed her away with his demeanor.

Later that evening he was his old self again, though, and neither of them said any more about that strange moment.

⁂

"Hey Tony, look at this."

In the days that followed his surprising outburst, Tony had been the same loving man as before, and Greta decided it was just a fluke... a crazy bad mood. Everything was okay again. She leaned over the back of his chair, put her arm around his shoulders, and placed the folded newspaper in front of him.

"Do you think we could go to this open-house tomorrow?" she asked with excitement.

Tony shoved the newspaper away from his face, knocking it out of her hands. "Jesus, Mary, and Joseph," he snapped. "Now we're house hunting?"

Greta's jaw dropped and she stepped back in surprise. The newspaper floated to the floor as Tony jumped to his feet and started pacing around the room. His hands were balled up tight.

Greta watched then moved toward him. She reached out to touch him, but he pulled away and drew back one fist.

Greta flinched.

Tony's face turned pale. He dropped his hands to his side, and his eyes filled with tears.

Greta's next words were barely audible. "I just thought..."

"That's the problem, Greta! It's what you're thinking!"

"What's wrong, Tony? What's happening?" Greta's voice was shaking with the fear that coursed through her. The words that followed hurt more than a physical blow.

"I'm sorry, Greta, but you're smothering me! This just isn't working. You know I care about you," Greta saw the pain on his face as he spoke, "but I've got to get away. I can't do this anymore."

There were more tears, and more words that Greta wouldn't remember afterwards, and then he was gone. The emptiness he left overwhelmed her. She sat in silence staring at a shadowbox hanging on the wall.

Once again she was alone.

☙❧

Greta held the phone in her hand. She dialed Tony's number. After one ring, she hung up and put the phone down. Walking to the window, she stared out at nothing.

"I need coffee," she said to no one. "I won't sleep anyway... might as well." The coffee smelled comforting and the mug felt warm cradled in her hands. She settled back on the couch and flipped through the TV channels... then turned it off. Greta looked at the phone, reached for it, but stopped. With a sigh she picked it up again and dialed his number.

Maybe he'll answer this time, she thought.

"Hi, this is Tony. Can't get to the phone right now. Leave a message and I'll get back to you."

"No, you won't," Greta sighed as she hung up.

There will never be another love in my life like ours, Tony, she thought, *but I can't just sit here alone night after night.*

Greta grabbed her car keys and headed out the front door.

Chapter 3

Autumn 1995

Aunt Kim's eyes were cast down at her dinner plate. It would be another quiet and lonely meal for Greta since Bobby was out with friends again.

At the head of the table, Uncle Don seemed oblivious to everyone and everything except the slab of meat he was cutting and stuffing into his mouth.

Greta knew she should be grateful—after all where would she be without them? All the same, she felt nothing for either of them and longed to be back with her father and Grammy.

Her thoughts went back to the days before her grandmother died... before life with Uncle Don and Aunt Kim.

"Greta, would you please finish clearing the table?" Grammy asked. Greta's excitement grew.

"Yes, ma'am!" She knew this signaled time for birthday cake and presents. She was right. By the time the last plate was in the sink her grandmother was lighting the tenth candle on her cake with her father standing by her side. They sang Happy Birthday.

"Blow out the candles, and make a wish," Grammy said.

Greta blew them all out with one big breath and smiled in satisfaction. Then came the presents. The new clothes were nice, and the books, but most of all she loved her sketchpad and colored pencils.

"Daddy, look! Now I can make lots more pictures."

"Sure you can." Her father's smile gradually faded, like it always did, and he gathered up the torn wrapping paper and left the room.

"Grammy, why does Daddy always get so sad?"

"Well Greta, when your Mama died, a part of your Daddy died with her." Putting her own grief aside, with a warm hug, Grammy always let Greta know how much she was loved.

"Greta, eat your dinner," Don Taylor's gruff voice interrupted her thoughts. "C'mon girl, quit your daydreaming and eat."

She picked up her fork and took another bite of roast beef. It was dry. *Aunt Kim sure can't cook like Grammy did,* she thought.

To Greta, her Grammy Pamela Margaret Sanger had been the most wonderful woman in the world and the only 'mother' she'd ever really known.

Until she too was taken.

They had been driving to the shore, and Greta was excited about the prospect of spending two whole weeks playing in the sand and surf, eating seafood in all the familiar seashore restaurants, and going to the boardwalk in the evenings. Greta loved the sights and sounds and smells. It had been a family ritual for as long as she could remember and one that she liked as much as Christmas morning.

Grammy was in high spirits and even Dad seemed less serious and distracted. It was the only time she ever saw him truly relax.

Driving down the highway, Greta was lost in daydreams while Gram and Dad chatted in the front seat.

"Do you think our rooms will be ready when we get there? We're making such good time, we'll probably get there by two o'clock." Her grandmother hoped they wouldn't have to wait.

"Probably," her father answered hopefully, "since check-in's normally at three. I think we'll have time to get out on the beach for an hour or so before dinner."

Greta had no memory of what happened next. But when she woke up in the hospital, her life had changed forever.

"Her vitals are getting stronger." Greta could hear two people talking, but she couldn't understand. "This is going to be tough. How do you tell a child something like this?"

"I think she's waking up."

Who are they talking about? Greta struggled to open her eyes, but they were so heavy.

"Greta… Greta, open your eyes, hon."

Why is she yelling? Greta's head hurt. Everything seemed to hurt… and she started to shake. She felt someone pull the cover up over her arms.

"It's okay, hon. You're okay. Open your eyes."

Greta blinked. She tried to speak but her mouth was so dry.

The woman who had pulled the blanket up, smiled. "Nurse, would you get her some ice chips? Greta, my name is Dr. Henderson. This is Julie, your nurse."

But why are you here? What's happening? Greta looked up with fear-filled eyes.

"You were in an accident, but you're going to be all right, hon. We'll take good care of you." Greta accepted the piece of ice Julie placed in her lips.

"But… where's Grammy?" she croaked. "Where's Daddy?"

Dr. Henderson tried to comfort her as she broke the news. She explained that another car had hit theirs.

"Your father and grandmother were hurt very badly."

Greta felt the tears begin to slide down her cheeks. She wanted the doctor to stop talking. *No! No… we're going to the beach.* She remembered that but nothing more.

Eventually she learned that her father and grandmother were killed on impact. She wanted to scream and cry and kick and make these people stop saying such awful things. Greta didn't move.

"There must have been an angel watching over you, little one," the nurse said later. Miraculously, Greta had no life-threatening injuries.

How can that be? What's going to happen to me?

For the first few days after Greta woke in the hospital she was just numb. Then came the fear, the terror. *Who's going to take care of me?*.

"Greta, if you're finally finished eating, take your plate into the kitchen… and bring me a cold beer." Her uncle pushed his chair back and headed to his favorite spot in front of the TV. Greta did as she was told and was relieved when she could finally escape to her room. She took out her grandmother's rosary and laid across the bed.

It's just not fair. I need you, Grammy, Greta thought. *How could you leave me?* A little later, she dried her tears, and still holding the rosary slid off the bed and onto her knees. Her grandmother's words echoed in her brain. *'Always say your prayers before you go to sleep, Greta. God is always listening. God answers prayers.'*

"Dear God, please help me to be good and not to do anything to make Uncle Don mad. God bless Aunt Kim and Uncle Don and Bobby. And God bless Grammy and Daddy." Tears began to flow from her closed eyes. She opened them and looked up toward heaven.

Why is this happening, God? Her folded hands curled into fists.

Chapter 4

August 2004

Greta drove aimlessly trying to escape the emptiness within those four walls... the emptiness that screamed *'Tony is gone... you are alone.'*

She finally pulled into a bar and lounge. *At least there are people here.*

"Let me have a wine spritzer, please." Finding three empty seats at the bar, she selected the one in the middle. The place was clean enough but obviously not too popular. It was practically empty. Greta looked at the rows of bottles behind the bar then caught her reflection in a mirrored sign. *I don't belong here.*

Before the bartender came back with her drink, she felt someone take the next seat and could sense he was looking at her.

Greta kept her eyes focused on the bartender, thanked him, and placed some money on the bar.

"Let me get that," the gentleman next to her said.

Greta finally glanced his way, trying to smile politely while declining. When her eyes met his, she saw an unshaven, grimy face that held an ugly proposition. This was no gentleman.

"No, thank you," she said almost inaudibly, and, "Excuse me..." Trembling, she grabbed her purse, left the untouched drink, and hurried from the bar.

She jumped in the car, locked the doors, and checked the rearview mirror to be sure he hadn't followed her out. She fumbled to get the key in the ignition. Successful at last, Greta took one more look in the rearview mirror before speeding away.

The following Friday evening, with the fiasco of venturing out alone still fresh in her memory, Greta was glad to be having dinner with her best friends. Maria and Freddie always lifted her spirits.

"Thanks for having me, Maria. Something smells delicious!"

"Freddie's in the kitchen and everything's just about ready." She took the bottle of wine Greta brought and headed through the dining room with it. "I hope you're hungry."

"I am... and that aroma is making my mouth water." Greta looked at the dining room table. It was beautifully set with four place settings. Greta's eyebrows shot up. "Is someone else coming?" she asked. Maria wore a sly smile when she answered.

"Well, yeah. I thought... I mean Freddie has this friend, Terry, and he's a really good guy," she talked even faster than usual, "and, well, we figured it wouldn't hurt for you to meet him... and it's just dinner, yanno." She peeked through her lashes to see Greta's reaction. "And besides, he's really good-lookin', girlfriend! Just wait..."

Greta smiled. "I can't be mad at you," she laughed, "even though you're so sneaky." She wanted to ask more about this mysterious guy, but the doorbell interrupted them. Greta peered over Freddie's shoulder as he opened the door.

"Hi Terry, come on in."

Greta saw a tall, blond-haired, blue-eyed, good-looking jock type with laughter in his eyes. She was impressed.

"Nice to finally meet you," he said taking her hand. "I've been looking forward to it."

So I'm the only one who wasn't in on it, Greta thought as she shook his hand and murmured her greeting. They were soon gathered around the table enjoying casual dinner conversation.

"Where's Ariana this evening?" Greta asked.

"She's having a sleepover at Tia Brenda's tonight. Her cousin enjoys being the big four year old that can make the baby giggle. And we get to have a nice dinner with no interruptions." Maria laughed, "Now who wants me to cut their meat for them?"

Laughter was followed by lots of good food and conversation, and everyone was able to handle their Arroz con Pollo without Maria's assistance after all. And there was more to come.

"Is everyone ready for the Tembleque?" Maria asked pushing her chair back from the table. Greta read the mystified look on Terry's face and decided to help him out.

"It's a kind of coconut pudding," she said. "Trust me, you'll love it... and there's always room for Tembleque." She was right, and it was the perfect dessert to finish off the meal.

It was Greta who finally suggested it was time to call it a night after draining her third wine glass.

"Well, it's getting late. I should probably be going." She had seen the secret looks between Maria and Freddie and knew they must be looking forward to some alone time with Ariana away. "Freddie, do you mind?" Maria had promised Freddie would take her home.

"Sure, let me get my car keys."

"Wait," Terry interrupted, "may I drive you, Greta? Then these love birds can..." he hesitated, "well, you know... whatever," he chuckled.

So that's why Maria insisted on picking me up. Greta shot a glance at her friend that said 'I know what you did.' Then thinking of no objection, agreed.

On the ride home Greta thought about what a good evening it had been. Maria, Freddie, and Terry even had her laughing by the end of the night. She almost forgot how lonely she was until Terry walked her to the door. She dreaded the loneliness waiting for her inside.

Greta once loved her first little apartment, but now it felt more like a place of solitary confinement. She didn't want the evening to end. On a sudden impulse she turned to Terry and invited him in for coffee.

"Well, maybe just for a while. Can we make it an Irish coffee?" She liked his smile. She wanted his company.

It was nearly an hour later that she walked him to the door and he turned to kiss her goodnight. Greta took a step toward him, and escaped into his embrace. Terry seemed surprised when she fell into his arms but didn't object.

She later worried what he must think of the woman lying next to him. But even though embarrassed, at least she was safe from the emptiness... for now. Greta pushed the guilt away and hoped she might finally get her wish.

܀

Apparently Terry wasn't scared away by my incredibly brazen ways.

He stayed with her nearly every night for the next eight months. Greta liked seeing his blue toothbrush there next to hers even when he didn't stay over. She wasn't alone.

They laughed and played together like two carefree kids, eating outlandish amounts of wonderful food in all the best restaurants, hiking, biking, sailing, and lying on the beach that summer. It was all fun, and it seemed it might go on forever. Forgotten were those ugly, dark days and nights of desolation.

It was one of those lovely, lazy summer evenings. Terry was tending the steaks on the grill, and Greta brought out a cold beer for him along with her glass of iced tea. Everything else was set on the patio table and ready to go so she sat down as he brought the sizzling steaks from the grill.

"Here ya go, gorgeous." He put a steak on each of their plates, reached for his beer, and sat down across from her.

"They smell wonderful," Greta said. "I knew I didn't love you just for your looks and sparkling personality. You can cook too!"

Glancing up, she saw a strange expression cross his face.
What did I say?
Oh...

Neither of them had said those three words out loud in all the months they'd been together. It just kind of slipped out. She hadn't planned to say it. But there it was.

"I do love you, Terry," she said more quietly, looking into his unreadable expression and waiting for the expected response.

The silence that followed was deafening. It took only seconds for her to realize he wasn't going to say it, to realize he hadn't wanted to hear it, to realize her wish was going up in smoke again.

As quickly as it had begun, it was over.

"Gr...Greta," he stammered. "You know I love spending time with you. We have such a great time together. Let's not complicate it, okay?"

"Sure, yeah, just forget I said that." She laughed it off in spite of the icy feeling running down her spine. They enjoyed the rest of the evening, and Greta knew he wasn't staying tonight because of a scheduled work trip. But she was surprised when she got ready for bed.

The blue toothbrush was gone.

Chapter 5

1995

Kim and Don Taylor lived on the other side of Baltimore, but it could have been the other side of the country for as often as the extended family got together.

Aunt Kim was her father's sister, a timid, quiet woman, and her husband Don seemed okay, but he didn't say much. He usually looked like he'd rather be somewhere else. He was always the first one to say, "Well, we'd better get going."

The two families only got together on holidays and special occasions… like weddings and funerals—and God knows there'd been too many funerals in Greta's short life—but she didn't feel like she knew Kim, Don, or their son Bobby at all.

Yet there they stood telling Greta she would be coming to live with them. She was to be discharged from the hospital in a couple of days, and she knew she couldn't go home to live in her old house alone at the age of ten. She wasn't sure what to think, but knew she should be grateful to them for taking her in.

When that day came, Greta dragged her feet and looked helplessly back at the kind nurse's warm smile.

Greta felt no such warmth on the drive back to her new home.

Aunt Kim and Uncle Don only had one child. Bobby was fifteen years old. He was entering his sophomore year in high school, and Greta was just in fifth grade. In a couple of years he'd be going off to college. Her aunt and uncle wouldn't have had any children tying them down if it weren't for the niece who was forced on them.

Greta felt like a guest—an outsider—for a long time after she moved in with them, but eventually the days and the routines became more comfortable. She had plenty to eat, a nice room. Greta had her dolls, and she watched TV. But she was lonely. She missed the feel of Grammy's arms holding her close. No one in this house ever gave hugs like that.

At night she cried, muffling the sound in her pillow.

"How was your day, sweetie?" Grammy asked even before Greta hung up her coat.

"I got an A on my math test, and I got to read my report, and everybody clapped when I was done," Greta answered all in one breath. She hugged her Grammy then grabbed a seat at the table to help her snap beans. *"And guess what else... Jenny's having a birthday party, and I'm invited! Can I go, please?"*

Greta's grandmother laughed. *"We'll check with Daddy, but I'm pretty sure it will be all right. I guess we'd better think about a present for her then. Do you know what she'd like?"*

"Sure, she's just like me!" Greta grinned. *"Can we go shopping for something Saturday?"* Greta chattered on and on, but her grandmother never seemed to mind.

Greta missed her Dad too, in a way that was different and hard to explain. She just missed his presence. Even though he'd been so sad and distant, he was there. He was her Daddy.

"Sleep tight, pumpkin," he said as he kissed her goodnight. He sat just watching her. *"I see your Mama in your eyes, Greta. She was beautiful, you know, and she loved you so much."* He seemed to be about to say more, but instead brusquely kissed her goodnight. As the door closed behind him, Greta wondered what he'd been about to say.

But that part of her life was over. Daddy and Grammy were gone and all she had now were her memories. Through her tears Greta asked, "God, why did you take them away?"

Greta turned to her sketchpad. Grateful for that long ago gift, she could see her grandmother's love looking back from the page. The drawings of her father were more difficult. She struggled with the eyes and could never seem to get them just right. But her father and grandmother were gone.

Now her Aunt and Uncle had taken their place. Aunt Kim didn't have the warmth of Grammy's eyes, and Uncle Don...? Well, Greta simply didn't understand him at all.

Sometimes he'd come home from work all jolly and playful, teasing Aunt Kim and Bobby, and even trying to include her. Other nights he'd be sullen and cross and everyone in the household walked on eggshells to keep from saying the wrong thing.

Like the others, Greta learned to tiptoe around his moods when he might lose his temper over the littlest things... like the night Kim served roast beef and scalloped potatoes.

Taylor took his seat at the head of the table and looked over the dishes before him. "Where are the mashed potatoes?" His tone screamed disapproval. He glared at Kim who cowered in her seat.

"I thought you might like these for a change," she said softly reaching for the bowl of scalloped potatoes. Don Taylor stood up, knocking his chair to the floor.

"You know damn well I want mashed potatoes with roast beef. This is bullshit!" He stormed out of the room.

Greta saw her aunt flinch as he passed. Kim sat frozen, head down, appetite gone. The refrigerator door slammed and Greta saw Uncle Don head for the den, beer in hand. He would drink his dinner.

Bobby stared down at his plate as he ate. "Mom," he spoke barely above a whisper, "the potatoes are really good." He ate a few more bites then asked to be excused.

After Greta helped clear the table, she finally escaped to her room. On the way, she passed by Bobby's partially opened door and saw him lying on the bed with his headphones on. He had his own way to escape.

To Greta, Don Taylor's moods were strange and frightening that first year. But she'd soon learn—his moods weren't the worst he could do.

Chapter 6

June 2006

When Greta and Tom were introduced, there was an immediate attraction, and they had such fun together. They ate, danced, laughed, cuddled, and enjoyed each other from the beginning, and it seemed it would go on forever.

Greta was sure of it this time.

Unlike Tony and Terry, Tom said he was ready to settle down. They'd moved in together after just four weeks of dating. Of course, they were intimate even before that.

If she hadn't learned anything else in her earlier years, Greta had learned that was what men expected.

It was their one-year anniversary of moving in together, and Greta took special care applying her makeup, She chose the sapphire blue dress Tom loved on her, brushed out her hair, and wore the pearl-drop earrings and pendant Tom had given her on her birthday. She was checking the pork roast when she heard Tom's text-tone on her cell. Her heart sank as she reached for it, already anticipating what it would say.

```
Sorry will be late. Working on case. Don't wait
dinner.
```

Tony's law practice kept him at his office for long hours, and once again his work came before her. Greta wanted to hold dinner until he got home. He'd been late a lot the last few weeks, and he'd call or text, insisting she should go ahead without him. He never knew how late he would be.

She tried to call, but it went straight to voicemail. He probably didn't even know how special this evening was to her.

Greta fixed two plates, one for herself and one that she could pop in the microwave for Tom when he got home. She set up a tray in the living room in front of the TV, not wanting to sit alone at the table again, and began to eat. The dinner which she had looked forward to was now tasteless. After pushing the food around her plate, she finally carried it back to the kitchen and scraped what was left into the trash.

Tick, tock, tick tock... The clock in the hall mocked her as the hours passed and she tried to stay awake.

This case he's working on must be a real doozy.

Her head jerked... fighting sleep but losing the battle. The 11:00 p.m. news was on. Maybe it was the utter boredom or perhaps the stress of being alone, but she was exhausted and decided not to wait up for him any later.

However, sleep did not come easily. Greta was finally dozing off when she heard Tom get home. Lying quietly, she heard him soundlessly crawl into bed next to her after 2:00 a.m. She rolled toward him, but Tom turned to face the other way. He lay still and quiet until just moments later his usual snoring told her he was asleep.

ॐ

Opening her eyes and stretching, Greta glanced at the clock on the bedside table. Eight thirty-five. Rolling over and not finding Tom by her side, she realized she could hear the shower running. That was what must have roused her from a restless sleep.

Why in the world is he up so early after having such a late night? The water shut off, and she could hear him shaving before finally opening the door and greeting her, "Good morning, sweetheart. Sorry about last night."

"Good morning," she smiled up at him. "Did you heat up your plate when you got home? I'm sorry I didn't hear you come in," she lied.

"No, that's okay. I wound up taking my client to dinner. We had some points we had to discuss before we decided if this is worth taking to trial."

Greta felt old suspicions constricting her heart and wondered again if they were groundless—or if she was a fool.

"You're up awfully early, Tom. Aren't you exhausted? When did you get home?"

"I'm afraid it was kind of late. What time did you go to bed?"

"I had a long day so I turned in around 10:30... just couldn't keep my eyes open." Greta hated lying and knew she was baiting him, but she had to know.

"Oh, I'm not sure exactly when I got in, but I don't think it was much later than that. Anyway, I feel great, and I'm hitting the links... got an early tee time." Tom reached down, giving Greta a quick peck on the cheek and heading through the bedroom door called back, "I'll just grab something at McDonald's on the way. See you later!" and he was gone.

Greta sat on the side of the bed stunned and disappointed. This felt too familiar. And not a word about their anniversary. *He's lying, and I'm losing him,* she thought. *Maybe I should have realized that it was getting later and later and more and more frequent.*

After Tom left, Greta reached for comfort with her caramel cream coffee, took a shower, dressed, and headed outside with her second cup of joe and no particular appetite for breakfast.

Always desperate to be in a relationship, Greta hated being alone. Lately that's how she felt. *What good is it to be in a relationship if I'm still always alone?*

When Tom finally came through the front door, Greta screwed up her courage and was ready to confront him. After a short greeting Tom excused himself to go freshen up and returned to find Greta sitting on the couch with a glass of white wine. There was a cold beer sitting on the coffee table for him.

"Ah, just what the doctor ordered," he said reaching for the beer with one hand and the TV remote with the other.

"Tom, could we skip the TV for now and just talk for a while?"

"Well, I was going to check and see how my team's doing, but okay. What's up?" he asked turning toward her. Greta tried to read his face but it was closed, no emotion, just innocently blank.

But is he innocent?

"It's no big deal," she started, "but you've been working such long hours, and then with your golf, it seems like we never have much time for each other lately. It gets lonely rattling around in this empty apartment all the time."

"It's not *all* the time, Greta. Seriously, why do you have to make such a big deal out of everything? Work is work, and can't a man relax with a game of golf on the weekend, for God's sake?"

Greta was shocked by the vehemence in his response and suddenly finding herself on the defensive.

"I'm sorry," she said almost inaudibly, "it's just that I miss you. I mean I miss our time together. Please don't be mad."

He just looked at her, shook his head in disgust, and grabbing his beer, went out on the deck and flopped into one of the lounge chairs.

Greta sat, not knowing how to undo the damage she'd done. Finally, she opened the slider and joined him on the deck.

It was a pleasant, cloudless afternoon and should have been delightful sitting there with the man she loved, but she could only see the clouds on Tom's face and, though the words raced through her mind, she couldn't spit them out.

Clearing her throat to break the silence, she began again, "I'm sorry I've upset you. I just meant..."

She was cut off before she could finish as Tom spat out, "Jesus Christ, Greta, you're always sorry about something. Would you just drop it?"

Though she was offended by such language, she swallowed her objections. She sat quietly... and listened to the silence cementing the wall between them.

Chapter 7

Summer 1997

    Uncle Don was a car salesman. He managed the dealership, but to Greta it seemed all he really did was sell cars. She didn't like car salesmen very much. They had an overly friendly manner that didn't feel quite right.

    Greta learned that her Uncle Don was like that... all friendly and nice as long as everything was going his way. But it was really all about *him*. Without warning he could change into a cruel, cold-hearted tyrant. If he didn't get his way, everyone paid. Greta learned that lesson well... eventually.

    There were times when Greta began to like her Uncle Don—a little—like when he took her to his dealership.

    "Do you want to stop and get a hotdog on the way home, hon?" he asked taking her hand and leading her to the car.

    Greta hesitated before answering. She loved Coney Island hotdogs, but it was awfully close to dinner time. "Do you think Aunt Kim will be upset if we spoil our appetite?" she asked.

    "Don't you worry about your Aunt Kim. This will be our little secret," he winked. "She doesn't need to know everything."

    Greta finally agreed. She did love those hotdogs... but she felt kind of guilty the whole time she was eating it.

    Uncle Don ruffled her hair when they finally got home and was in a good mood all evening. Everyone seemed happy. Her aunt relaxed and smiled at her husband, and he even smiled back.

    "Did you have fun going along to the dealership today?" Kim asked Greta.

With a quick glance at her uncle, Greta caught his wink and nodded nervously. She said nothing about her special treat, and wondered why she felt so uncomfortable.

Her own father had never spent as much time with her or been nearly as affectionate. Yet Greta knew her daddy loved her. She had seen it in his eyes.

But she didn't see that in Uncle Don's eyes.

Bobby was away at college now, and Aunt Kim would be gone for hours getting groceries on Saturday afternoons. Don Taylor talked to her about boys and how she must learn never to trust them. Greta didn't understand what he meant at first, but he said they would tell her how much they liked her just so she would do certain things.

It was all very confusing.

Another Saturday afternoon, just a few weeks later, he began to show her what he meant.

She was sitting on his lap at the time. He liked to have her sit on his lap, and although it wasn't like the warmth she remembered sitting on Grammy's lap, it did feel good to have that contact. She felt safe. She felt loved. She didn't feel so alone.

He affectionately rubbed his hand up and down her arm. Feeling contented, it was almost like when Grammy held her so long ago. She felt safe and warm. She felt loved. A gentle sigh said maybe things would be okay.

Greta suddenly froze when her uncle's hand slid down over her shoulder and touched her breast. She had only just begun to develop, and was quite excited about finally getting boobs, but now she gasped and started to pull away.

"Shh, shh. It's okay, Greta," he reassured her in a whisper. Paralyzed with fear, she didn't move. "Relax, sweetheart. I'm your uncle. You know I'd never do anything to hurt you. You know that, don't you?"

Did she know that? Greta was confused and overwhelmed with strange feelings and unfamiliar sensations.

"I just want to show you what you have to watch out for with boys," he said. "You see, this is what they're going to want to do, but they won't love you the way I do. They just want to touch you."

He was speaking in such a quiet, gentle voice; there was a gentleness she'd never heard there before.

"It's okay, sweet little Greta, it's okay. I'll never do anything to hurt you. You can trust me. But this is just between you and me, okay? Your Aunt Kim's kind of funny, you know, and she just wouldn't understand how I need to help you."

Greta would never forget that day, the way her body betrayed her, and the beginning of a secret life that separated her from the rest of the world.

Chapter 8

October 2006

Wandering around the empty apartment aimlessly, Greta wondered what was wrong with the men she chose. They always seemed so charming. Smart. Responsible. They'd had good jobs, a good sense of humor, and most importantly, they'd fallen in love with her… or so it had seemed.

But could that really be love?

If you really love someone, how can you just walk away?

All the same they did walk away.

Well, Tom practically ran, and what he left behind was a crumbling mess of estrogen-loaded tears.

Enough, Greta thought, *no one will ever hurt me like that again.* She finally accepted, men just couldn't be trusted.

Greta thought back to that final straw. Tom had obviously just been waiting for the opportune moment, an excuse to walk out and blame her for the demise of their relationship, but it was obvious he already had one foot out the door before she'd said the words that gave him permission to let the rest of his body follow.

"Tom, I think we need to make some changes. We're getting to be more like roommates than a couple. I think I deserve more that. I think we both do."

Tom was out of his seat like he'd been ejected and, with a veil of contempt, said, "Well, good luck with that."

She had practiced her speech but never even got to the part suggesting they go to counseling. Greta found herself staring at the door that had slammed as he went out, and sat in stunned silence with his words reverberating in her brain.

The following day when Greta got home from work, she returned to find his side of the closet and his dresser drawers empty. Of course the golf clubs were no longer leaning in the corner next to the door either. The only new item was a note on the dresser with his forwarding address. Apparently, he'd known for a while he was leaving since he already had other living arrangements made.

Greta looked at the empty spaces. *What's wrong with me? Is it the kind of men I'm choosing, or is it something about me that drives them away?* She opened and closed his dresser drawers, slamming the bottom one in disgust.

God knows I do everything I can to please them and make them happy. Didn't I learn to make potato salad just the way Tom's mother did? She stared out the window and saw nothing.

Wasn't I there waiting for him whenever he walked in the door? I never made plans to do anything without checking with him first.

But this one had ended just like the others. The apartment was deadly quiet, and the loneliness weighed her down, but she also felt angry, and with that anger came a new resolve. Greta made a decision that day. She put aside the dreams of a big wedding, the children, and the life she had always hoped for, and put all of her energy into her career. *All pipe dreams! It's time to get real.*

The quiet was painful so Greta turned on the TV. The news might be depressing, but at least there was the sound of other voices though she barely followed what they were saying.

"Let's see," she said out loud. "Shall I have the mac and cheese, the Salisbury steak, or the rice and beans? Yuck! None of the above." Instead, she opened a can of minestrone and made a grilled cheese sandwich. It didn't really matter what she ate. Nothing had any taste.

At least it was an easy clean-up after. *Now what?* she wondered. *Hmm, I think I still have some ice cream.* She scooped out a generous serving of fudge ripple, carried it back to the living room, and mindlessly ate in front of the TV.

Well, that was pretty good, she thought, *but if I keep this up I'll be shopping for a new wardrobe in bigger sizes.*

Greta felt restless and reached for the phone to call Tom out of habit. *Don't be a fool!* she thought. Reluctantly, she put the phone down and wandered into the kitchen. She looked in the refrigerator, opened cabinet doors then closed them again.

There was nothing in the kitchen that could satisfy the hunger of loneliness.

Ten minutes later Greta turned off the TV, grabbed her jacket, keys, and purse and headed out the door. She had no idea where she was going. She just had to get out of the townhouse for a while.

She'd loved that apartment from the moment she and Tom had walked in the front door. They'd made a lot of good memories there, but now they were just ghosts and demons haunting and taunting her. *I need to get out of here before I become one of those ghosts.*

Backing out of the driveway in the last light of day, Greta drove to the corner, took a left, and headed for the Beltway. It wasn't until she'd been driving for fifteen minutes that she realized she was heading for Maria's house.

Maria and Freddy were parents now. They'd had a beautiful baby girl a little over two years ago, and here was Greta, alone again, no boyfriend, no babies, no life.

Pulling into their driveway, Greta saw them inside. The lights were on, and they hadn't pulled the curtains closed yet.

What a delightful little family. They've got it all. What do I have? Nothing! Greta watched them through a blur of tears. She reached to put her keys back in the ignition, not wanting to drown in their happiness, when the front door opened and Maria came over to the car. The concern in her eyes said it all.

"Get in here, woman!" she said. "Freddie's taking Ariana up for her bath so we can talk. You poor thing." She guided Greta into the house and straight to the kitchen where she reached for the Chardonnay and a couple of glasses. "Tell me about it, sweetie."

Greta found shelter in her friend's arms, and with that Greta's dam of tears broke.

Chapter 9

1998

Greta sat with her sketchpad, her only escape, and watched as the pencil moved. Her Grammy's face began to appear on the page before her. She thought of the times she'd sat on her Grammy's lap to watch TV. They hadn't watched a lot of television back then, but she felt warm just thinking about being on her Grammy's lap, giggling at the cartoons or whatever they were watching. There was safety in those arms, and there was love—so much love.

And then it was gone... in the time it takes to draw one breath, it was gone.

Aunt Kim was kind to Greta when she'd moved in. She never really said a cross word, but she also never held her on her lap. She didn't read to her or laugh with her as they baked cookies together like Grammy had. Greta knew Aunt Kim did her best to take care of her, but she just never let her in. She remained just the nice aunt who took care of her.

Greta turned the page and drew quickly. When she was done, she looked at the scene—a young girl stood alone—the woman across the room from her looked away. *She never really looks at me. It's like I'm not here...* Greta crumpled and tossed the page into the trash. She stared at a new, blank page.

Uncle Don, of course, was another story. He held Greta on his lap; he wanted to be close to her, to love her. Or so he said. But there was no feeling of being safe and warm when Uncle Don had her sit on his lap. No. Only fear and confusion and guilt. Her fist tightened around the pencil in her hand.

He didn't usually pay much attention to Greta at all when Aunt Kim was there. It was when they were alone that he became so attentive.

Greta started asking if she could go with her aunt to the grocery store. And she did get to go sometimes. Aunt Kim thought it was nice that Greta wanted to help. But Uncle Don would be in a sullen mood when they got back, and more and more often wore the smell of beer that went along with his sour mood and quick temper.

Greta saw that her aunt didn't understand the reason for those moods, but then she'd always seemed afraid of her husband's quick temper and had long since given up trying to understand.

Eventually Aunt Kim must have discovered a connection between taking Greta with her and coming home to his pouting behavior. So Greta's trips to the grocery store became more and more rare and time with her uncle more and more frequent. Greta learned to dread Saturdays.

Greta loved to draw beautiful things. But when Saturday came, and Aunt Kim drove off to run her errands right after lunch, Greta was left alone with him... and her drawings changed.

Greta tried to stay busy, saying she had to finish cleaning her room or work on a school project, but try as she might, it usually ended the same way. If she avoided Uncle Don long enough and Aunt Kim got home before he had his chance to do what he wanted, he would be angry and cruel to both of them. But if he got his way, he was sweetness and light—treating Greta like a princess and even being kind to his wife.

It was so much nicer when he was like this, but the cost was her innocence. Greta felt guilty if she let him do what he wanted. She felt guilty *and* responsible if she didn't... and they all paid the price. Greta learned if there was to be peace in the house, no matter how she felt about it, it was up to her to pay in advance.

After dinner, she withdrew to her bedroom and her sketchpad. Sometimes the pencil seemed to have a mind of its own and Greta mindlessly allowed it to flow. The muscles in her neck and shoulders relaxed. She was at peace with her art.

Greta saw the rocking chair appear on the page. The pencil flew faster as Grammy seemed to appear with open arms. Then with harder, darker strokes the figure morphed into her Saturday nightmare. Her grip on the pencil tightened with shock as she saw the result. The resemblance to Don Taylor was uncanny. His face was hard. There was no love in those sinister eyes.

Greta was appalled. She tore the page out and began ripping it to shreds. She tore it until the pieces were mere confetti falling to the floor with her tears, and she silently screamed, at someone.

I hate you! I hate you!

Chapter 10

Late October 2007

"Hey Maria, what are you up to this weekend? Wanna meet me for lunch and do some shopping?" Greta spoke hopefully into the phone.

"Oh, I'm sorry, girlfriend. I forgot to tell you, Freddie has to work today and I promised Ariana a playdate with her cousin." Greta's smile faded. "You could come along if you want. I'm sure Brenda wouldn't mind."

"No," Greta laughed, "you have fun. I should probably clean out my closet, anyway. How about tomorrow?"

"Oh man, I can't. This guy Freddie works with invited us to have dinner with him and his wife. We're heading to their house right after Mass. I'm not sure what time we'll get home... but do you want me to call you when we do?"

Greta heard Maria's worried tone and quickly reassured her. "No, no, don't be silly. I'll probably do a little shopping, and then I have a ton of paperwork to catch up on," she lied.

When the call ended, Greta stared at her phone wondering how she would fill the long empty hours. The quiet apartment seemed to scream, "You have nothing to do and no one to do it with." She reached for the remote and flipped through the channels. *Well, I guess it's just you and me, Rachel Ray.*

Monday morning finally arrived, and Greta was happy to be heading back to work.

Everything was backwards lately. She looked forward to her work as a distraction from her ever-present companion—loneliness. The dreaded empty weekends came too quickly and lasted too long.

Thank goodness for Maria. But then Greta felt guilty for not staying in touch until she'd needed her. Greta had a bad habit of being so wrapped up in the current man in her life that her world shrank.

So this morning Greta showered, dressed, did a quick make-up and hair, and took off for work. She drove purposefully through the city to her downtown office.

At age eighteen she'd struck out on her own with only a high school education and sheer determination to be independent. Greta was still determined not to need anyone to take care of her.

A high school education didn't open many doors in the marketplace, but Greta was able to find a job in a local department store. She'd started as a sales clerk and before long proved she was a responsible employee who could be depended on to go the extra mile. Never late, Greta arrived at least a half-hour before her shift, and was willing to stay late when needed. She had a friendly, pleasing manner with both customers and fellow employees. Before long Greta was given more responsibility and began taking business classes at one of the local community colleges. Teachers had always said she was a bright student who grasped things quickly and this proved to be the case as she climbed the corporate ladder.

Greta wasn't heading for a department store this morning, but for the corporate offices downtown where she now held a prestigious position for such a young woman. There were plenty of empty spaces in the garage at this early hour. She parked and took the elevator to her office on the seventh floor.

After hanging her Burberry in the closet, she indulged in a gourmet French vanilla coffee and took a moment to enjoy the view of the city. Then she settled down to tackle the paperwork that awaited her attention.

Her secretary wouldn't be in until close to nine o'clock so Greta left the door to her office opened. Not that she was expecting anyone. Early mornings were the best part of the day. No interruptions!

So she was a little surprised when the door opened and a stranger stepped into her office.

"Hi, I'm Gabe Engel. I have a nine o'clock appointment," said a man with twinkling blue eyes and a charming smile. "But you don't look like a Mr. Gibson."

Greta met him with a polite smile and said, "No, are you sure you're in the right place? What office were you looking for?"

"Sheppard Technology Systems."

"Oh, okay, Mr...?"

"Engel, Gabe Engel."

"Okay, Mr. Engel. You need to go up one floor and go to the end of the hall, through the glass doors. I think it's the first or second door on the right," she explained.

"Thank you, Miss...?"

"Friedman, Greta Friedman," she smiled, stood, and extended her hand. *Why am I offering to shake his hand?*

"Thank you, Miss Friedman... Greta. Very nice meeting you, and my apologies for interrupting your morning. Have a good day and thanks again." His eyes fairly danced as he smiled and backed out the door.

Strange, Greta thought. *He looks bright, but my door clearly doesn't say Sheppard Technology Systems.* But she hadn't minded the interruption. *Too bad his appointment wasn't really with me!*

Greta grabbed another cup of coffee. After the night she'd had, she was going to need a caffeinated day.

Chapter 11

Spring 2002

Uncle Don kept 'teaching' Greta about boys.

His lessons included 'what they want' and how he was 'protecting' her. Greta felt more helpless and hopeless the longer it continued. She cried night after night and prayed for it to stop.

But it didn't stop. Taylor became bolder.

She held her breath when he crept into her room late at night. *Maybe if he thinks I'm asleep, he won't touch me...* But he did.

"Please... no..." she begged in a whisper as she curled into a fetal position on her side. But his hands found her.

"Shh, you have to be quiet," he breathed in her ear. He leaned in closer and whispered, "I love you, Greta."

With clenched fists she submitted. He pushed his hand between her legs, and the tears fell onto her pillow. Greta bit her lower lip hard. She couldn't let Aunt Kim hear. *Why, God?*

Uncle Don warned her that if she ever told, no one would believe her. He said everyone knew Greta had mental problems because of the accident. But Greta knew that unless she told someone soon, she really would go insane.

One morning after Uncle Don left for work, she lied and said she was too sick to go to school. She was a high school senior with almost perfect attendance, so Aunt Kim didn't doubt her word. Greta went back to her room and spent the next hour working up her nerve.

She found her aunt sitting in the living room watching a game show. "Aunt Kim, can I talk to you for a minute?"

"Oh honey, shouldn't you be in bed?" she answered too quickly.

"Actually, I'm not really sick. I just stayed home because I needed to talk to you alone."

A look of apprehension crossed Kim's face. Greta instantly knew this wasn't going to be easy for her aunt to accept.

She looked as frightened to hear what Greta had to say as Greta was to say it. The woman on the couch shriveled before her. Greta watched her aunt's body push deeper and farther back into the sofa, trying to distance herself from whatever was about to be revealed. Kim's head dropped, and she intentionally avoided eye-contact. *Just like she does when Uncle Don's on a bender,* Greta thought.

"It's about Uncle Don." Her aunt looked away not wanting to hear anymore. Greta forced herself to go on, searching for the right words. "He, um, he does things... I mean, he's been... touching me..." Her voice cracked and she felt the blood and shame rushing to her neck and cheeks.

"Stop it, Greta! Don't be ridiculous. You're just a child. You don't understand him." Shocked by her aunt's reaction, she stood silent. The seconds felt like minutes. Hours. She searched for her voice.

"But, it's true. I mean... what he's doing, it's not normal. It's not right." She swiped at the tears that came unwanted.

"No! Your uncle is just trying to make you feel like part of the family. He feels sorry for you because you lost your father," Kim said a little too loud. Greta's tears burned. She saw the anger in her aunt's eyes.

"But Aunt Kim, you don't understand. He touches me in my private places," she cried.

"No, stop it, Greta! I don't know why you're saying such things, but stop it! Go to your room... now!" Greta looked into eyes full of anger... or was it fear?

Greta's own fear turned to terror, and in panic all she could think to do was escape.

Chapter 12

Late October 2007

The morning went by quickly. After her secretary arrived, Greta became completely absorbed in the tasks before her and lost all track of time. Kathy had been working for her only a few months, but had become indispensable. With someone to answer and screen calls, Greta could scratch one thing after another off her to do list.

A rumbling like distant thunder erupted from her mid-section and told Greta it was time to grab some lunch. She looked at the clock on her desk. *Quarter 'til one. No wonder I'm hungry.* Of course her mind had been so muddled that she hadn't even thought about packing a lunch. *Looks like the little coffee shop in the lobby will have to do today.* Greta grabbed her Coach bag and headed for the elevator.

As the doors began to close behind her, a man's voice called, "Hold the elevator," and he jumped on.

Greta looked into the twinkling blue eyes she'd seen just a few hours earlier and saw that same charming smile. Gabe Engel obviously recognized her.

"So we meet again," he laughed.

Greta replied with a few pleasantries as they rode down to the lobby together. She had to look up when he spoke and guessed he must be at least six feet tall. He didn't look as though he spent much time outdoors, or if he did, he wore sunblock. Greta noticed he had beautiful skin but pulled her eyes away when she realized she was staring.

Exiting the elevator she headed for the coffee shop and realized he was walking along the same route. She glanced his way and was embarrassed to see he was glancing at her as well.

"Are you getting lunch, Ms. Friedman? And if so, may I join you?"

Greta's previous interest plummeted. *Just like Uncle Don warned...*

He must have seen the look of suspicion in her eyes.

"Sorry, that must seem like a cliché pick-up line. It's just that I don't know anyone here. I'm from Pennsylvania, by the way. I only thought it would be nice to have someone to share a quick lunch with."

Well, I guess that makes sense, but...

"I'm sorry, Mr. Engel was it? But I was just going to grab something and have a bite to eat at my desk."

She saw the disappointment in his eyes and decided it wouldn't hurt. *It's just lunch after all.*

"Well, I guess it might do me good to take a break." She smiled realizing she would really like a little conversation... a little distraction... a little human companionship might be refreshing.

This man is a perfect stranger. He could be a mass murderer for all I know. She laughed at herself, and the amusement must have slipped onto her face.

"Can you share?"

"What?" Greta asked.

"What's so funny? I'm sorry, you just looked like... never mind."

Greta wondered if gold flecks gave his eyes that twinkling look or if he just had an amusing secret hidden there.

"Oh no, just thinking... um... let's see what kind of soup they have today," Greta deflected.

After ordering and picking up their lunch, Greta led the way to a table. She intentionally sat across from—rather than beside— the stranger who had suddenly popped into her life, both amused and intrigued by him. It wasn't that she was attracted to him. She was still reeling from losing Tom. That wound was too fresh to even think about another man.

"What's wrong, Ms. Friedman?" Gabe asked.

"What? Oh, call me Greta, please. No, nothing wrong, why?"

"Sorry. I didn't mean to pry. You just looked like something was bothering you. Forgive me. It's none of my business."

Greta felt an unfamiliar urge to share her thoughts but stopped short. Why in the world would she start blabbering about the most intimate problems in her life with someone she'd only just met? Someone she knew absolutely nothing about?

"Sorry, I just have a lot on my mind. You know, work stuff." Greta shrugged it off thinking it really wasn't his business. "So, how about you? You said you're from Pennsylvania?"

They talked about the things people often discuss when getting to know each other... kind of like cocktail party conversation.

Greta found that she almost hated to head back upstairs to work, but their plates were empty, as were their coffee mugs, so it was time.

"Well, thanks for the company, Mr. Engel."

"Gabe. Please, call me Gabe. 'Mr. Engel' is my father," he laughed. "And the pleasure was mine."

After an awkward goodbye, Greta went back to work but found herself thinking about Gabe. *Too bad I'll never see him again. He seems like he'd be a good friend,* Greta thought. *That is, if a man and a woman could ever really be just friends.*

Chapter 13

Spring 2002

Greta ran back to her bedroom in tears.

"Don't say anything to your uncle about this!" Kim yelled. "He'll be furious if he finds out. Then we'll all pay!"

It had taken every bit of courage Greta could muster to finally reach out for help, but Aunt Kim had none to offer.

Greta threw herself on the bed and cried as the panic grew. The only other sound she heard was the soap-opera drama playing in the other room. Greta had enough drama of her own. Aunt Kim didn't even come to check on her.

Determined to escape, Greta grabbed a bag, threw in some clothes, pictures of her family, her toothbrush and toiletries, the red sketchpad, and her grandmother's Bible and recipe box. Sniffing repeatedly she paused just long enough to get a tissue and blow her nose.

When she got to the bedroom door, she saw the shadow box hanging on her wall. It was filled with memories from family trips to the beach… including a favorite conch her father found as a child. Carefully lifting it off its hook, Greta added it to her few precious possessions.

Grabbing more tissues and her school bag, Greta looked around at the room that had never become home to her. She wouldn't miss the ugly rose-colored carpet or the mismatched furniture.

She tiptoed from her bedroom, looked at the back of her aunt's head, and wondered if she would be okay. She couldn't see the dazed look in Kim Taylor's eyes as they watched the TV without seeing. Greta regretted leaving her to deal with her husband when he got home, but she knew she had to go.

What will he say when he finds out I told? What will he do?

With growing panic she rushed through the kitchen to the mud room. A quick glance at her drawing of a ship on a stormy sea, hanging above the coat hooks made her catch her breath. Aunt Kim, lost in her own thoughts, didn't hear Greta quietly leave by the back door.

Greta didn't know where she was going, what she would do, or where she would stay. She just knew she had to get away. She ran like the girl in her nightmares—only this time she was awake with no alarm clock or morning sun to set her free.

Greta had carried her secret alone, too afraid to tell anyone what her uncle had been doing to her. Now she had nowhere to turn.

She walked quickly in the general direction of her school until, out of breath and exhausted, she collapsed on the steps of St. Matthew's. After she caught her breath, Greta looked up at the doors of the church and saw her answer. She'd come to the one place she always felt safe. Greta fell on her knees in a pew near the altar and allowed the tears to come.

She'd been raised in the Catholic Church, though they didn't attend regularly. When she'd gone to live with her aunt and uncle, she'd stopped going to mass at all because the Taylors didn't go. But she used to take out her grandmother's rosary faithfully each night before bed. Until she'd become angry with God. Night after night she'd knelt by her bed and begged for his help, but He never answered her prayers.

Now, in utter desperation she was back to ask for His help once more. She had no one else to turn to.

Praying and shivering with cold and fear, she felt someone sit down next to her in the pew. Greta looked up into the concerned face of a young priest.

"What is it, child? I don't mean to intrude, but I saw you crying. Is there something I can do to help you?" he asked.

Inexplicably, Greta forgot her fear of telling and poured out the whole ugly story to the young priest.

"It's not your fault, child," the priest said as he offered her tissues that he seemed to pull from nowhere. "You've done nothing wrong."

"But..." Greta began.

"No, Greta, no buts. You are not responsible. This is not your sin." He looked sorrowfully into her eyes. "If you'd like, I can hear your confession, but you must leave the guilt behind."

It was much later, after giving her absolution, that the Father said, "Now, I'd better call your aunt and let her know where you are and that you're okay."

Greta's eyes widened with fear. "No, please. You can't tell her. She'll tell my uncle and..." Looking for an escape route, Greta pushed away from the priest, ready to run. Not knowing what to say. Not knowing what might happen. Knowing only fear.

Seeing her panic, he was persuaded to wait and agreed to take her somewhere safe. Greta was only weeks away from her eighteenth birthday and months away from graduation. Father O'Connor gave in to her pleas and decided to take her to the home of two of his married parishioners to stay until he could figure out what to do next.

Settling Greta in the rectory kitchen with Mary, who fixed her some soup and a grilled cheese sandwich, the Father placed a call to the Martins, a middle-aged couple who had raised two lovely daughters and were charitable in every way.

Father O'Connor didn't go into detail about why Greta had left home so suddenly. He simply explained that she was in great need of a place to stay for a while. Knowing the Father wouldn't ask this of them if the child hadn't been desperate, they agreed to take her in for as long as she needed. The Martins, Greta would discover, were a generous, loving couple, and they tried to make her feel at home with them.

Yet Greta felt more alone than ever.

Chapter 14

Late October 2007

    Several days went by, and Greta's thoughts kept going back to Gabe. She tried to shake it off because she knew she'd never see him again.

    Thursday afternoon on the way home from work, Greta stopped by a new little market she'd recently discovered. Recognizing her diet was seriously lacking, it was time to start eating healthy and taking care of herself. The crowd of people buzzing around was a good sign. Greta slipped the brown shopping basket on her arm and joined the throng.

    She started with red, yellow, and orange peppers. Drawn by the fragrance she chose fresh basil, rosemary, and thyme. Greta found she was actually getting her appetite back, and the throng of people somehow lifted her spirits.

    "Aren't these bananas beautiful?" a little gray-haired lady exclaimed. "At the store where I usually shop they're always too green or way over ripe." The woman reminded Greta of her Grammy as she put a small bunch in her bag and moved on.

    Greta smiled at the memory and grabbed a few bananas and oranges for herself. With her basket full of beautiful greens, oranges, reds, and yellows, Greta had only one more stop. Making her way to the meat counter, she almost walked right into the man with the twinkling eyes.

    Startled and flustered, Greta wondered what it was about those eyes that was so magnetic.

    They both laughed. "So we meet again, Ms. Friedman."

"No, it's Greta, remember? And Gabe, right? Fancy running into you!" she laughed, surprised at how delighted she was to see him standing there.

"Ah," said Mr. Twinkle Eyes, "it must be fate. Looks like you're planning a real healthy dinner tonight."

"Yes, I've been eating way too much junk lately. Time to get back to eating right! Would you like to join me?"

Oh my God, she thought with utter mortification. *What the hell am I doing? I just invited a perfect stranger to come back to my place for dinner! I must be losing my mind!*

"Wow, thanks Greta. That's kind of you, but I really wasn't trying to wrangle an invitation to dinner. I have a business meeting at 7:00 this evening and don't know how long that might take."

"Of course, that was silly of me to ask," she stammered. Greta dropped her eyes. *How could I have been so stupid?*

"Not at all," he said, gently lifting Greta's chin. "It was nothing but kind and sweet." When their eyes met, Greta felt a jolt of electricity jump from his fingertips to her very core. "And I'd really love another opportunity to spend time with you. Would you consider dinner tomorrow night?"

Greta's heartbeat quickened. She didn't know if she should say yes or run for her life.

This is moving too fast. What am I doing? She felt her head nodding in agreement even as she wondered if she was once more heading down a path to heartbreak.

"Great! I'll let you pick the restaurant since you're a lot more familiar with them than I am, okay?" Greta saw nothing but sincerity in those mesmerizing eyes and agreed. "Thanks, Greta. Being away from home it gets pretty depressing, eating out alone or grabbing junk at the fast food places. How about if I give you my number and you can call me with the details?"

Greta began to relax. She put his cell number in her phone and promised to call him the next day about time and place. Dinner in a public place certainly made more sense than her original impulsive suggestion, and she was grateful to him for suggesting it.

Back in her car a short time later, Greta pulled into traffic still thinking about Gabe. Though she knew little about the stranger, she already felt she could trust him.

As she signaled and turned right at the light, a smile settled on her face.

She didn't notice the white Ford Taurus that had pulled out behind her as she contemplated the chance encounter with Mr. Engel. Her mind was totally occupied by the intriguing newcomer in her life.

Gabe had told her a little about himself Monday during their quick lunch. She knew he was new to the area having moved here from Pennsylvania and that he was single. Her smile widened. He was a consultant, contracting in the area of business and technology, and he worked a lot with Human Relations and team building for the companies that sought his services. Right now he was working with a company in her building, where he had been heading when he'd shown up in her office by mistake.

A lucky mistake, she thought with a chuckle.

Reaching her home, Greta pulled into the driveway, and the white car swerved around her and sped off. *What an idiot*, she thought. *Everybody's in a hurry.*

Carrying her parcels into the house, she felt the usual emptiness as she glanced around the kitchen. Everything was just as she'd left it that morning. She flipped on the overhead light and looked at the single coffee mug sitting where she'd left it... where there used to be two.

The answering machine showed zero messages. Greta put her bags of produce on the bare counters and cursed the answering machine holding silent vigil. She didn't need to press the button to know Tom hadn't called.

Shaking off the oppressive feeling, she got busy right away cleaning and storing broccoli, peppers, mushrooms, and all the other goodies from the market, and then changed into her sweats before fixing dinner.

She picked up some chicken and decided on a quick stir-fry. Cooking hadn't been one of her talents when she first went out on her own, but over time, trying to please the men in her life, she'd gotten better. Greta enjoyed watching Rachel Ray, Paula Dean, Rocco Dispirito and many of the other chefs on the cooking network, and she'd bought more cookbooks than any one person really needed.

It had been fun trying new recipes and having Tom try them. He really liked her cooking and fortunately wasn't a picky eater. Stir-fry was one of his favorites.

Thinking about Tom, the stir-fry lost its taste.

Chapter 15

2002

"Margareta Karlyn Friedman." Hearing her name, Greta walked across the stage and accepted the diploma and warm handshake from the principal. *I did it, Daddy!* She knew he and Grammy would be so proud if they were there. But the only people at the ceremony for her were the Martins and Father O'Connor.

Greta was surprised to find balloons, decorations and a beautiful cake when they all got back to the house. The Martins were always so thoughtful and kind. But Greta couldn't stop thinking of her Dad and Grammy.

"Graduating with honors! That's quite an accomplishment, young lady. Congratulations," the priest said.

Tears filled her eyes. She tried to hide them, but Father O. saw and understood. He gave her a gentle hug and whispered, "I know... it's hard." Greta took a deep breath and smiled at everyone.

"Thank you. This is so nice."

"Just look at you... you're such a beautiful young lady, and you really should be so proud of all you've accomplished in spite of..." Mrs. Martin looked around awkwardly adding, "well you know, I mean it couldn't have been easy. So what are your plans now, dear?"

Greta knew she should be proud, but it was all so hollow. "I... I'm not sure," Greta stammered. "I mean..." she looked up helplessly. "I just don't know." She fought against the tears that threatened to fall. *What am I going to do now?* Her only desire at that moment was to fall into bed and pull the covers over her head.

"Well now, don't you worry," Mrs Martin patted her hand. "There's no rush. You know you have a home here for as long as you want." Mr. Martin nodded in agreement

Greta knew they meant it. Whenever their daughters came to visit she was included in the family gathering. Theirs was such a warm and loving home. They were willing to have her be a part of it, but they weren't her family and that made her feel even more alone. And more cheated.

Greta stood among them, sometimes joined in with the talking and laughing, but all the while watched as through a window. Out in the cold isolation, she looked into and longed to be a part of it all... to belong.

Everyone told her she had her whole life in front of her, but she knew it had really ended in that terrible accident.

She just hadn't died.

※

Greta gave in to depression like never before. She was no longer living in survival mode, constantly trying to avoid being alone with Uncle Don. Now she was just alone.

She didn't have the distraction of friends at school to keep her going each day... so she saw no real reason to get up. She stayed in bed, sometimes all day, only ate what was lovingly forced on her by the Martins, and lost interest in everything.

At last, with Father O'Connor's insistence, she agreed to talk to someone professionally. She had talked to the young priest of course, but he knew she needed more help than he was qualified to give her.

Dr. Blair welcomed her into his office with a warm handshake and told her to have a seat in the chair next to his desk. Greta accepted, looking around at the warm brown and amber décor. It wasn't exactly what she'd expected. But then, she wasn't exactly sure about anything these days. Perhaps the notorious couch.

Hearing her name, she looked up to see the doctor's reassuring smile.

"I'm sorry. What was that?" Greta realized he had asked her something, but she had no idea what.

"I just wondered if you're comfortable. I know the first session can be a little nerve racking," he told her.

Looking down at her hands folded tightly in her lap, she lied. "Yes, I'm fine." She didn't feel fine at all. The brief grief counseling she'd had years before was a distant memory. Her anxiety was growing as she anticipated talking about those years with her uncle.

"Greta, I've gone over the intake notes, and I know you've experienced an awful lot for someone so young." He leaned forward and softly added, "Please take your time, and tell me about it."

"I'm not sure where to begin," she said barely above a whisper.

"You can start at the beginning, the end or even the middle."

The smell of his aftershave was familiar. She recognized it from somewhere. Then she knew. The memory of her father getting ready for work in the morning... that was the comforting scent.

"Greta, would it help if I asked you some questions first?"

"No, I'm okay, really."

Relaxing a little, she began to briefly recount the events of her early childhood. When she got to the part about the accident, her voice cracked. She looked across the room, and through the blur of tears noticed the painting on his wall for the first time. It was calming. A beautiful beach scene at sunset. They had been on their way to the beach the day her world fell apart. Taking a deep breath, she continued.

Dr. Blair listened to Greta's story that first session, and he heard her. She knew that he really heard her. That he understood her pain. She left his office feeling less alone. That day she began to trust a man, just this one man.

Maybe they're not all bad.

Over the next six months Dr. Blair supported her through the slow, agonizing process of moving toward acceptance. It was hard to say goodbye at the end of their final session. Greta wished she could go on seeing him every week. But he believed she had made as much progress as she could... for now. He promised she could call if she needed him, but he didn't think she would.

Greta was functioning again. She got out of bed each morning, showered, ate breakfast, and even started leaving the house. She had gotten a job and begun taking some evening classes. Greta loved to learn, and this was the best medicine for her malaise. Along with her business studies, she even took an art class. Art became a wonderful escape for Greta. Now she again had a reason to get out of bed each day.

But the nights were still a problem. She looked forward to Tuesdays and Thursdays when she had her evening classes. On those nights she was tired enough to fall asleep easily. Her sleep may have been restless, but at least she didn't lie awake for hours. Sometimes she fell asleep over her sketchpad in the wee hours of the morning.

☙❧

Greta was working in retail sales, not much of a challenge, but at least she was among people and making friends. She met her best friend, Maria, at the store. Stuck behind the Estee Lauder counter, which didn't always get a lot of action, Maria was doing makeovers just across the aisle.

Greta liked the way that, besides doing a great job with make-up, Maria seemed to make the women feel good about themselves. She chatted with the ladies, putting them at ease, and they always seemed to leave looking good, with their heads held higher and a bounce in their step.

Maria made Greta feel good, too. Especially the day when Greta had looked up and seen Morticia Addams' doppelganger across her counter and nearly burst out laughing. Maria must have seen what was coming and swooped in just in time.

"Oh, I love your hair!" Maria exclaimed as she interjected herself between Morticia and Greta. The young woman's face lit up. "You must really take good care of it. May I ask what kind of conditioner you use?"

Greta had quickly composed herself and was ready when her overly goth customer turned her attention back to the choice of a new lipstick. And she didn't miss the wink Maria tossed over her shoulder as she walked back to her station.

They had a good laugh later when they went on break.

"I knew you were gonna lose it, girl," Maria giggled, "as soon as I saw her walking toward your counter. You shoulda seen the look on your face!"

"Well, could you blame me?"

Maria laughed harder. "Yeah, I sorta wanted to offer her a makeover, but I don't think that's what she was looking for. But boy, she sure coulda used a little blush!" Maria rolled her eyes and the two young women rolled into a friendship Greta would learn to cherish. Maria could always make her smile and sometimes even forget her loneliness—at least until she crawled into bed at night.

Greta also met a boy. His name was Todd, and he was very attentive. He asked her out. He was nice. He said he loved her. And she, being so starved for love, believed him. Todd used her for a while, tired of her, then threw her away.

I guess Uncle Don was right, she thought bitterly.

Greta was devastated, and her loneliness was magnified a million fold. But she was an attractive young girl, so there were other guys. Soon she found another boyfriend. This one lasted longer, but eventually it too ended.

The next couple of years saw boyfriends come and go, each with the same devastating result. Sunday afternoons on Maria's couch… hours filled with gallons of ice-cream, cookie dough, chick-flicks, tissues, and tears. Each time left her more humiliated, filled with self-doubt, even self-hatred.

Greta continued with her night classes and proved her worth at the store. She became an invaluable employee. Her excellent work ethic, intelligence and skills, along with her enviable people skills resulted in one promotion after another. She had learned early in life the importance of pleasing people. She'd honed this skill to perfection.

As a people-pleaser, Greta was loved by all... as long as she kept on pleasing.

Chapter 16

November 1, 2007

Greta called Gabe midmorning and suggested Sabatino's for dinner. It was on Fawn Street, not far from the Inner Harbor, and had great Italian food and a lovely ambiance, especially with the piano playing soft dinner music. She was never disappointed in the food, and they served a great bubbling Moscato. They agreed to meet at the restaurant.

Greta left work early and headed home for a refreshing shower then looked through her closet, not sure what to wear. This wasn't a real date, or was it? Greta sat on the side of the bed not knowing exactly what she felt, why she was going to dinner with this guy, or what she expected. Well, whatever it was, it was better than sitting home alone on Friday night feeling sorry for herself.

Enough tears had been shed. She realized there was no chance she and Tom would be getting back together. They weren't married so there were no complications with their split up—no children, the townhouse was in her name, and he walked away not wanting any kind of settlement. It was crystal clear. Although they'd never married, Greta had gone through an emotional and physical divorce.

Greta was looking forward to dinner with her new friend.

Beats the hell out of sitting here feeling sorry for myself for screwing up my life!

She decided on a soft, copper-colored dress, simple gold necklace and drop earrings, and a cute pair of brown patent pumps.

Checking her reflection, she was satisfied. Her looks had never been the problem.

A few minutes before 7:00, Greta got out of her car and walked into Sabatino's. To her delight, Gabe was already there waiting for her, and from the approval in his eyes, she saw she had hit the mark. He smiled in greeting.

"Our table is ready." He led her to the table set for two, and pulled out the chair for her before taking his seat. Greta smiled in appreciation. It was nice to be treated like a lady.

The menu was familiar to Greta so when Gabe asked what she'd recommend, she suggested several dishes she thought he'd enjoy. They ordered a nice bottle of her favorite wine. Salads were delicious and conversation easy and informal. Greta found herself relaxing with this easygoing stranger.

By the time the main course arrived, the mood was one of old friends.

"How's the scallopini?" Gabe asked casually.

"It's good," she answered, "really good. I almost always get the veal parmigiana, but decided to try something different." The parmigiana had been Tom's favorite.

Greta found Gabe easy to talk to, and as the evening went on she found herself sharing more about her recent breakup. He listened attentively. His eyes as well as his words showed he understood and cared. Gabe didn't spout the usual trite expressions people offer in an attempt to comfort and make the problems go away.

"That had to feel like a kick in the teeth. I'm sorry you had to go through that. Sounds like Tom didn't deserve someone like you."

Greta looked into his eyes and knew it wasn't just a line. She knew he meant it.

By the time the dessert menu was brought around, Greta felt self-conscious and wondered if she had said too much. She had certainly done most of the talking.

They lingered over their cannoli and coffees until she realized the hour and suggested they should be going. She sensed Gabe would have let her go on talking forever.

As they stood to leave, Gabe smiled and pointed to a table where four men were enjoying dinner. "I see a very good friend of mine over there. Do you mind if we just stop and say hello?"

"Not at all," she replied.

As they approached the table, recognition lit his friend's face. The two shook hands.

"Greta, this is my very good friend, Dr. Shane Farrell. Shane, Greta Friedman."

Shane extended his hand. Greta couldn't help noticing how attractive he was and immediately scolded herself.

Gabe walked her to her car. "May I follow you to be sure you get safely home?"

It felt good to be looked after. Instinct told her he had no ulterior motives. When Greta pulled into the driveway, Gabe got out of his car and walked her to the door.

Oh God, here it comes. She held her breath waiting for him to ask to come in… not knowing how to respond. *Maybe he is just like the rest.*

He stopped and asked, "Are you busy tomorrow? I was thinking, if you're free, maybe we could go to the Aquarium at the Inner Harbor."

Greta realized he wasn't going to ask what she'd expected. Unaware she'd been holding her breath, she finally exhaled.

Gabe continued, "I've heard Baltimore has one of the best. I was going to go alone," he continued, "but it would be a lot more fun if you'd join me… that is if you're not busy."

Greta's mind reeled with the unexpected invitation. "I…I actually was going to do laundry," she stammered. Her hesitation suddenly seemed foolish even to her. Laughing, she added, "No, wait. Okay, it's a date!" She wanted to take those last words back, but they were already out there. Embarrassed, she asked, "W…would you like to come in?"

The invitation felt awkward, but Greta didn't want to be rude by saying good night and leaving him standing there.

"No, it's been a really long day." Gabe smiled and took a step closer. I'd better be going, but can we meet about 10:00 in the morning?"

Greta braced herself for his attempt to kiss her good night, not knowing exactly how she felt about it. Instead he smiled down at her and took her hand in both of his.

"Good night, Greta... and thank you." Gabe turned and walked back to his car. He waved then stood by until she was safely inside.

I don't know if I'm relieved or offended, Greta thought. She watched from the window as he drove away.

Chapter 17

November 2007

The black Mustang pulled up to Greta's curb at 7:00 a.m. Taylor felt pretty rough after his binge the night before and the fight he'd had with his wife at 3:00 in the morning, but he had dragged himself out of bed because he knew he must. His wife didn't hear him leave the house, and he didn't care about the swelling on the side of her face. He had more important things to take care of.

Chapter 18

Greta awoke the next morning amazed that she had fallen asleep so easily the night before. She didn't remember any tossing or turning; there were no tears. Her mind had just been going over the events of the day, wondering what the next day would hold.

She'd also slept later than usual. It was almost half past seven, and she was to meet Gabe at the harbor at ten o'clock so she hustled herself out of bed, and after a refreshing shower headed for the kitchen for a light breakfast and coffee. She was looking forward to the aquarium more than she first realized.

She hadn't been there in years, but that wasn't the only reason. She knew she wanted to see Gabe again, with his warm smile and ever twinkling eyes. There was something almost magical in those eyes. Not like anything she'd ever known before. Somehow those eyes said everything would be okay. She felt love in them. Not what she'd had with Tom. Not the passionate love she'd felt with Tony. No, this was different. She didn't quite understand it, but she craved it.

By ten o'clock Greta was searching the crowds for his smile. She'd dressed carefully once again, in a casual but attractive pair of jeans and a sweater. She was still able to get away with just a jacket, but the air was definitely getting cooler. It would soon be time to pull out the winter coat.

As she approached, Greta saw Gabe waving, smiling as usual. His smile drew her in. She approached with the same anticipation as when she'd been a child walking home from school, to find Grammy waiting in the kitchen with fresh baked cookies. *Now you're just being silly, Margareta,* she thought. *I doubt Gabe has any cookies in his pockets.*

Gabe and Greta got their tickets and walked into the aquarium together like old friends rather than new acquaintances. He seemed genuinely delighted as they meandered along. She wasn't sure when he'd taken her hand in his, but she liked the warmth of it. And the comfort. *He's just what the doctor ordered to treat the gloomies.*

"What are you smiling about, Miss Greta?" Gabe asked.

"Oh, was I smiling? I guess I'm just enjoying myself more than I expected."

"Ah, I see," he replied. "So you thought I was really going to be a bore, eh?"

"No, no," she laughed, "not at all. I just haven't enjoyed much of anything lately, you know, since the break-up. But this was the perfect idea. The fish are so beautiful," she smiled up at him, "and the company's not bad either."

He laughed out loud. "Glad to hear it."

ॐ

When they finally left the Aquarium, they were famished and headed over to the many little restaurants lining the harbor area and decided on one with great seafood.

Greta ordered her favorite soft-shell crab sandwich. Gabe raised his eyebrows when the waitress set it on the table in front of her.

"I'm glad I went with the shrimp salad sub. I'm not sure I'm ready for a sandwich with little legs sticking out the sides of the roll."

She laughed with him, "Oh, that's right. You're not from around here." Greta was surprised at how easily the laughter came when they were together.

"Just not sure about something with big old spider legs. I'll have to take you up to Pennsylvania sometime to try some of our dishes. How does Hog-maw sound to you?"

"Um, not great, but I'm willing to give it a shot." She winked as they laughed together.

"So Greta, you haven't said much about your family. Do they live here in the area?"

"Neither of my parents is living," she responded. "My mother died when I was a baby, and my father and grandmother, who helped raise me, were both killed in a car accident when I was ten."

"I'm so sorry, Greta. Well, then what happened to you? I mean, who took care of you after that? Or am I being too nosey? I don't mean to pry or make you uncomfortable."

Strangely, it was easy talking to him about it, but she stopped short of going into detail about Aunt Kim and Uncle Don. They weren't a part of her life anymore, and she was quite happy to leave it at that.

"I'm sorry they hurt you," he said quietly. Greta was taken aback. She hadn't said anything about them hurting her. Yet she felt no need to deny it.

"How did you know?" she asked.

"It's in your eyes. When you spoke of them a cloud came over your face. I could see that it pained you just to think about them. I'm sorry; it sounds like you didn't have an easy childhood."

Even she heard the bitterness in her voice as she remarked, "Yeah, you could say that. But let's not spoil a perfectly lovely Saturday afternoon going down that road. I'd much rather hear more about you."

"Not a whole lot to tell. Normal childhood, parents who loved and took care of me. Oh, they got a little obnoxious when I was going through my teen years and didn't know much, but the older I got, the smarter they became!" They both laughed, and he went on, "They're living down south now and enjoying some relief from Pennsylvania's winters."

"Will you be going to spend Thanksgiving with them?" Greta inquired.

"No, not this year. The project I'm involved with right now definitely won't be done that soon, and I can't take that much time away. What about you? Where will you be having Thanksgiving dinner this year?"

Greta hadn't thought about it until that moment and suddenly realized she had no plans. She would have been going to Tom's parents' home to spend the day with his family if they hadn't split.

"I hadn't really thought about it," she admitted.

"Well maybe we can go get a hotdog together or something," he winked.

Laughing, she agreed that might be a plan. She wasn't sure about the hotdog, but the 'or something' definitely had possibilities. *I might have something to be thankful for after all.*

Chapter 19

Kim Taylor sat curled up on the couch staring at the TV, totally unaware of what the reporter was saying on the eleven o'clock news. Her thoughts jumped around like so many frogs in a pond. They jumped mainly from fear to anger and back again, wondering what was in store for her when her husband finally got home. He would be drunk, of course. Her hand reached up to touch the side of her face. She didn't need a mirror to know it was swollen and bruised.

There had been no phone call, but then she wasn't expecting one. He never bothered to call anymore.

He'll just come home whenever he damn well pleases... and he'll reek of beer, she thought and then wondered if she would be his punching bag again tonight. He didn't hit her too often, but it had gotten worse after Greta left, and last night had been one of the worst. Don blamed his wife for letting the girl get away.

"Like it was my fault," she said aloud. "I'm not the one who drove her away. Damn you, Don Taylor! Maybe she was telling the truth that day. And now I'm paying the price. You bastard! I wish you'd just wrap your damn car around a tree and I'd never have to look at your face again."

Chapter 20

A week after their trip to the aquarium, Greta and Gabe had dinner with Maria and Freddie. Greta watched her best friend and her husband chat casually with Gabe. They liked him.

Maria asked, "So what are you guys doing for Thanksgiving?" She smiled across the table at Gabe and Greta who glanced at each other. Their silence was all Maria needed to hear. "It's settled then," she laughed. "You'll have Thanksgiving dinner with us!"

Gabe's smile faded as he looked around the table, eyes landing on Greta. "Oh, I forgot. I sort of told Shane maybe the three of us could go out on Thanksgiving. You remember Shane, Greta? Dr. Farrell? I introduced him to you at that Italian restaurant. He has no family here in Baltimore either," he said apologetically.

Greta remembered the dreamy looking doctor quite well.

Without skipping a beat, Maria said, "No problem, bring him along!"

Freddie chimed in, "Great, do you like football, Gabe?"

"Does the sun rise in the east?" Gabe snorted.

With that it was settled, and the guys were off in a discussion of which team was the best… Ravens or Steelers… and which players were the greatest. The girls rolled their eyes and knew it would be a fun day, whoever was playing.

Greta and Maria got busy planning the menu. Greta would bring her baked corn, and Maria insisted she and Freddie would take care of the rest.

Greta, relaxed now, was glad she'd agreed to meet Maria and Freddie for dinner. She initially feared it was too soon to introduce them to Gabe… afraid they'd get the wrong idea of what was going on. Though exactly what was going on was still a bit of a mystery, even to her.

The last few weeks with Gabe had eased the pain of losing Tom. She enjoyed spending time with Gabe, but this was completely different from how her other relationships had started. Not that this was a relationship. Gabe had made no sexual advances at all. He would occasionally hold her hand or put his arm around her shoulders, and there had been a couple of friendly greeting hugs and farewells... oh yeah, and a kiss on the cheek. *Could he be gay?* Greta pushed the idea from her mind as silly and totally irrelevant.

Theirs was obviously just a platonic relationship, at least for now, and maybe that's all it would ever be. Maybe he didn't find her attractive. He treated her more like a little sister or a daughter. Greta couldn't help but wonder why.

The next morning Greta awakened to her cell phone's ring. She knew by the Latin rhythm that it was Maria, and she knew exactly what her friend wanted. Greta let it go to voicemail promising she'd call back after a shower, breakfast, and at least one cup of coffee. Forty-five minutes later, fortified by two cups of joe, Greta called her friend back and agreed to go to her house for lunch and conversation.

When she got to Maria's, she was already braced for the possible inquisition and probable scolding for moving too fast. She was prepared for Maria to warn her that her scars were too fresh to even consider getting into another relationship so soon. Greta was already prepared with her defense. After all, nothing was actually going on between her and Gabe.

Maria had instead opened the front door before Greta was even out of the car, and she was beaming. The friends hugged in greeting, and then Maria started in, but not the way Greta was expecting.

"My God, Greta, he's gorgeous! Where did you find this guy? I mean have you ever in your life seen eyes like that before? Wow!

I've got to tell you, girl, if I was looking, which God knows I'm not... I've got my Federico, but if I was? Oh yeah!"

Maria was laughing and to Greta's surprise, seemed utterly delighted with Gabe!

"So? Are you gonna tell me more? C'mon girl, I'm dyin' here! Fill me in... so what's happenin' with you two?"

"Nothing, Maria. Really, nothing at all." Greta smiled.

"No, seriously, I mean seriously? What is that? I saw you two last night and you were so perfect together... so easy. So, I don't know, like you just kinda belong there side by side. I mean those eyes... geez!"

"Maria, I swear, nothing's going on between us. It's been strictly platonic." With a bit of a smile she added, "Not that I'd necessarily beat him off with a stick if he did want more."

"Beat him off? Are you kiddin' me?" Maria exclaimed. "Holy Mother, you'd have to be crazy!"

Laughing, "Well hold on friend. You know Tom and I aren't actually ancient history."

Both women became more serious as they talked about the recent breakup and how foolish it would be to rush into another relationship—possibly on the rebound.

"That's what I always do," Greta said. "I've never been able to be alone for long."

"So then what's going on here, Greta? What is this with you and Gabe?" Maria asked.

"I don't know, but it's good. I don't feel like I have to get him in my bed," she said with a wink and a smile, "and I'm pretty okay with being home by myself most of the time. I mean I'm not as overwhelmed as before. I don't know where this thing with Gabe is going, but I'm pretty sure it's going to be all right. Let's just say it is what it is."

...But what is it? she wondered.

Chapter 21

Greta was sitting at her desk when she got the call.

"I know this might sound crazy, but the weekend forecast is for an Indian summer kind of day. Perfect for going out on the Bay. Are you game?" Gabe asked.

Greta hesitated for only a moment. It wouldn't be the first time she'd ever gone sailing in November.

She agreed to pack them a lunch and be ready early Saturday morning. A quick stop at the store got Greta home a little later than usual, and she was famished. She threw together a pasta casserole with lots of veggies and some red beans. It was a spin on a recipe she'd seen on TV and turned out to be delicious. After enjoying that with a nice glass of wine in front of the TV, she carried her dishes to the kitchen and loaded them into the dishwasher.

I really am okay, she thought. *I can do this*. It was getting easier to eat alone, to watch TV alone, and simply to be alone. Going to bed alone was still the most difficult part, but life in general was getting more bearable.

Greta wondered if Gabe was ever going to be more than a friend. It was all kind of confusing. She felt more for him than friendship, but it wasn't like the crazy, wild, passionate way she'd felt with Tony... or Terry.... or even Tom.

Well at least 'Gabe' doesn't start with a T. That's got to be a good sign. She laughed to herself.

Greta was drawn to him though. She looked forward to seeing him. She wanted to be with him. Maybe she just wanted him.

Drifting off to sleep, Greta's final thoughts were of Gabe. She floated into a dream of being in his arms as they danced round and round the ballroom floor. Sweet, heavenly music embraced them.

There was warmth, like bathing in sunshine by the sea. She looked up into his eyes and saw something beyond her understanding and heard his unspoken message repeated, *"Your dream is coming."*

Waking, Greta felt confused and annoyed. *What dream?*

Letting the water wash away the last cobwebs of sleep, Greta felt well rested and ready for the day, but her mind drifted back to the scene before she was so rudely awakened. Dreams were always fascinating to her when she remembered them, especially odd dreams like this one. They were rare. It was usually the nightmares that awakened her. This dream she didn't want to forget.

Next time I'll ask dream-Gabe what he means.

"Time to quit lollygagging," Greta admonished, sounding just like Grammy. After preparing the lunch, Greta returned to the bedroom and finished preparing herself. She dressed in layers since the mornings were so cool.

Like clockwork she heard Gabe's car pull into the driveway. She smiled at his punctuality and just because he was there.

They threw what they needed in the back of the car, hopped in, and headed for the bay. Greta was giddy with anticipation, but Gabe looked completely relaxed and turned on the radio.

They lapsed into a comfortable silence, enjoying the music. Greta slipped back into thoughts of her dream. She could almost feel the light of the dance.

Is my mind playing tricks on me?

"What's wrong?" asked Gabe glancing over at her quizzically. "Did you forget something? Are you okay?"

"No, no, I'm fine." she laughed nervously. "What is that music playing on the radio? Do you know?"

"I can't think what it's called, but it's Chopin. If you don't like it, I can put something else on, or you can look for another CD. I sometimes forget, not everybody likes classical."

"No, Gabe, I do like it. I think it's beautiful actually. I've never listened to a lot of classical music. I have to admit I didn't think it was too cool." She laughed again.

Gabe smiled. "I can find something 'cooler' if you'd like."

"No," she insisted, "this is fine... wise guy!" Then more seriously, "It's just that I'd never heard this music before, at least not that I remember, and now I've heard it several times, um, in a very short while." Greta's cheeks flushed with the memory.

Greta couldn't decide which was a more beautiful shade of blue—the sea or the sky. It was the most relaxing day she could remember since... well, she'd been at the bay with her dad and Grammy. She would have been content to float along forever.

Their conversation lulled as both she and Gabe seemed content to enjoy the soothing sounds of the sea.

"It sounds like I have a convert."

"What?'

"Chopin. You're humming the melody that was playing in the car on the way down here," he smiled. "So does that mean you like it, or is it just an 'annoying' tune you can't get out of your head?"

Greta felt flustered. She'd drifted back to the scene of her dream. "Oh, I'm sorry, I didn't even realize... I hope I wasn't annoying you. I'm not a singer!" She hoped he wouldn't pursue this conversation.

"Hey, don't put yourself down like that. You could sing with the angels."

Flustered by the compliment, Greta cast her eyes down.

"Looks like more clouds moving in from the west, and the wind's picking up. I think we'd better start heading in."

"Yeah," Greta agreed as she reached for her jacket. "It's a shame though. It's been such a great day. I hate to see it end."

"I know what you mean. There probably won't be any more days like this until spring."

Greta replied, "We'll just have to plan on coming back out the first really nice day of spring then!"

Gabe just smiled and turned the boat toward shore. His expression mirrored the darkening sky.

Chapter 22

Don Taylor tossed another cigarette out of the car window as he waited for Greta and the man she was with to return to the dock. He could see the dark clouds rolling across the sky and the gray curtain of rain they sent down to the sea. Bolts of lightning had been knifing through the sky in rapid succession, and he was glad to be safe and dry in his dealership car with a flask to keep him warm.

Greta hadn't even glanced his way as she sauntered onto the boat with her new beau. Her uncle knew he held the advantage using a different car each time he followed her. *That stupid little bitch doesn't have a clue,* he thought.

He wasn't sure how long he waited with only his whiskey companion. He saw several boats pull into the docks. He watched the people, mostly soaking wet men, make the dash to their cars, but still no Greta.

If their boat capsized in the storm, he pondered, *it would serve her right.* But he didn't want that. *No, if she's gonna die, I want to be there and watch. I want to be the one taking her down.*

Chapter 23

Gabe fought the sea as they headed toward the shore, but it would take at least an hour. The wind was picking up and the clouds were getting darker. It looked like they were about to get a summer storm in autumn. Greta was frightened, but tried to put her trust in Gabe and his ability to get them back safely.

The kind sea with gentle waves swaying their boat like a mother rocking her cradle now became more like an abusive parent. Gabe remained calm but totally focused on the task at hand.

The real fear for Greta began when she noticed a bolt of lightning followed quickly by its attendant rumbling thunder. She zipped her windbreaker and pulled her hood tight to ward off the soaking rain that was strengthening fast. All the warmth of the day had been sucked up into the gathering clouds and spat back down at them in increasingly heavy torrents. Greta shivered and held tight to the rails. She wanted to be closer to Gabe but was afraid to move.

The distant lightning now seemed to be all around them. The thunder was deafening. Greta had never been so afraid of the sea. Its beautiful blue water became a cruel black monster lurching them about, threatening to devour them.

Gabe glanced back at Greta and saw the fear in her face. "Come forward with me."

"I can't," she cried. "I can't!"

He held her gaze and called, "*Yes*, you can! Just look at me. Keep hold of the rails. You can do this. It's not as bad up here."

He couldn't let go of the wheel, and Greta was terrified. *How can he be so calm?*

"Greta," he called again. "Look at me... You can do this. Just keep looking at me and ease your way up... That's it... You're doing fine."

Greta kept her gaze on Gabe and fought to maintain her balance. She slowly pulled herself along the rail toward him. "Oh God, oh God, oh God..." she cried as she tried to keep her footing.

When she finally got close enough, she threw herself into Gabe's arms, almost knocking him off balance. By then she was nearly hysterical.

Gabe managed to get her in the seat up in the cabin area where she had some protection, but the water was coming from every direction. They were both drenched to the skin. Greta felt her stomach begin to lurch. When she looked across to the other side of the boat, it was pitched so high she couldn't see the water at all. And then it rocked so low the water appeared in a tower above it. She was sure they were going to capsize. She screamed, "God help us, God help us!" over and over.

Gabe kept looking back at her and fighting to stay on course. After what seemed like hours of combat to stay afloat, probably thirty minutes in real time, the rain slowed and came to a stop as quickly as it had begun. The sea still rolled, but the brightening sky brought hope. Greta's tears subsided with the rain, and she was left shaking and feeling sick.

Greta finally succumbed to the nausea and hung her head over the side of the boat. The waves were no longer the only thing heaving. "Be careful, Greta! Hang on!"

Somewhere in the back of her mind she knew she should be embarrassed—and would be later—but she didn't have time for that right now. She needed every bit of strength and focus to keep from going overboard. She would deal with the humiliation later.

All the times she'd been out on the water, she'd never been seasick before... but then she'd never been out during a storm. As the minutes passed, the bay grew calmer, and her nausea subsided. Greta thought how stupid they'd been to come out here in the middle of November. There had been other boats out with them earlier, but she only saw a couple now, and they were just about at the docks. Finally close to shore, she was flooded with relief and willed herself not to be sick again.

At last, they pulled into shore, docked, and quickly headed for the car. Sitting in the front seat, Greta and Gabe were the proverbial drowned rats.

They sighed with relief, looked at each other... and began to laugh. Gabe's laughter ebbed while Greta seemed unable to stop. She laughed until she cried, and then she was only crying. She was crying hysterically, in fact.

Gabe reached over and drew her to him. "It's okay, Greta. Let it out. It's okay."

When her tears finally subsided, Gabe slowly pulled out of their parking spot and headed back to her house without a word. He sensed how close she was to the edge and took her hand reassuringly. She could feel his strength.

They rode in silence until Gabe asked, "Do you want to talk?"

"No, I'm sorry. Not yet."

Respectful as always, he gave her hand a little squeeze, and she knew it was all right to just sit quietly. Physically and mentally exhausted, not yet ready to put words to the feelings, Greta was totally unaware of the black Ford Escape that pulled out behind them.

Chapter 24

Don Taylor's anger turned to relief when he finally saw one more boat heading for shore. He watched it dock under the clearing sky, saw the couple stumble off and rush to their car, and observed the tears of relief.

She was still alive. She could still be his.

As they started the car, and pulled out of the parking lot, he hit the ignition and pulled out at a safe distance behind them. He watched the other car merge onto the highway and followed until they took the exit toward Greta's home.

He let them go and continued straight ahead. *Not yet, girl. My time will come, but not yet.*

Chapter 25

When they finally got back to the house, Greta was still shaky, and her breath caught from crying so hard. Without asking, Gabe walked her in. He didn't say goodbye at the door as usual. Greta collapsed onto the couch.

"Would you like something to drink?" Gabe offered. She heard his offer through her fog and managed a slight nod.

Gabe brought her some water and sat down by her side. Greta felt numb.

After a few sips she managed, "There's a bottle of Moscato in the frig. Would you mind pouring me some?"

"Sure," he responded, "if I may join you." He brought them each a glass. "Now can we talk about what's really going on with you?"

Confused, Greta felt her anger rising. She wasn't sure where it came from, but she was angry. The fear Greta had on the sea pulled up the fears she'd lived with all her life... ever since she was an eleven-year-old child.

"I was scared, Gabe. I was so scared." Her voice quivered. "The storm and the waves... and I was so sick... it was all just too much."

"I know," he said, putting an arm around her shoulder.

Greta didn't want to fall apart in front of Gabe.

"Greta, tell me the rest of it," he said softly.

"The rest of what?" She was off the couch and pacing across the room. "My God, we could have died out there!"

"But you're okay now, Greta. Calm down... breathe."

"Calm down?" she heard the shrillness. "What are you talking about? Don't you get it?" The words tumbled out. She couldn't stop.

"Shh, shh, it's all right now." Greta focused on his voice and turned to face him with her chin quivering. Gabe took her by the shoulders. Feeling the tension, he gently stroked her arms. "It's over now."

Greta looked in his eyes through a blur of tears and crumbled. "Gabe, help me. Please help me."

"That's why I'm here, Greta."

"Just hold me."

She sat back down by his side, tears spilling down her cheeks.

He pulled her into the crook of his arm, but persisted, "Greta, tell me about it."

"What? Tell you about what?"

"Tell me about the pain. Who hurt you so badly, Greta?"

"Well, you know I just got out of a relationship..."

"No, Greta, who really hurt you? Who damaged you so badly that you can't get past it?"

Greta sobbed, wondering how he knew. It hurt so much. Then without warning the words tumbled out with all the fear and anger and hatred she'd kept bottled up for years.

She told him how she'd never really had a mother, how her father and grandmother had been taken from her, and how she'd had to go and live with her aunt and uncle.

She told him about Uncle Don teaching her about boys and what they wanted and how he had 'protected' her. She told him how she'd cried night after night and prayed for it to stop.

She told him about the day she finally risked telling Aunt Kim, hoping for help, and having her worst fears realized... how she'd run back to her bedroom with Aunt Kim calling after her, "Don't say anything to your uncle about this. He'll be furious if he finds out, then we'll all pay!"

Gabe sat quietly listening, holding her hands in his, as Greta recounted the events of the days that followed.

She told him how Father O'Connor had finally decided to talk to her uncle, and how he had denied the accusations until he realized the priest knew the truth and could not be dissuaded. Greta's voice grew bitter as she shared that the Father later told her Uncle Don had broken down and cried and begged him not to call the police. They had a long talk, at the end of which Don Taylor agreed to sign papers stating Greta could live with the Martins until her eighteenth birthday and that he would never try to contact her or in any way interfere with her life again. He did this in exchange for Father O'Connor not reporting the abuse.

Greta took a deep breath and went on, "The priest said, 'Just understand this, Mr. Taylor, I am speaking only for my own actions. If your niece decides to go to the police on her own, that's up to her. Keep in mind though, sir, that I know everything, and I will support her. I will testify on her behalf if it comes to that. And if I ever find out that you've broken our agreement, I guarantee you will be prosccuted.'"

Greta told Gabe how stunned she was the next day when Father O'Connor told her she was finally safe. She was relieved, but also upset. Why hadn't she done this sooner? Why had she stayed and let him keep hurting her... all those years?

She was overwhelmed with guilt and cried with shame. The young priest had told her, as Gabe was telling her now, that she had nothing to feel guilty about.

If only it was that easy... and if only she could believe she was really safe.

Telling it all, reliving it, Greta sat in exhausted silence. Gabe stroked her hair and she felt the tension begin to ease. Greta looked up at him with red-rimmed eyes reflecting a lifetime of sorrow.

"I think you've had enough for one day. Do you want to call it a night?" he asked.

"Yes," she sighed. "I'm so tired... Today feels like it's been a week long."

But Greta didn't want to be alone now that all those painful memories had been stirred up.

"C'mon, let's get you to bed." Gabe walked her into the bedroom where she sat motionless on the side of the bed. With his urging, Greta went into the bathroom and returned a few minutes later to see that he had turned down the covers.

She smiled with gratitude, standing where she was until Gabe took her by the shoulders and sat her back down on the bed. Though dazed, she wondered if he was going to kiss her... or something more. But seeing she wasn't going to move, he merely reached down and removed her shoes, and lifted her legs onto the bed. He gently laid her down and pulled the covers over her.

She started to object, to say something, but Gabe quieted her, "Shhh," and then she slept.

Gabe watched the pain dissolve from her face. She looked at peace lying there. As consciousness began to fall away, she heard Gabe's voice and something sounded so familiar... like a lost memory.

"Sweet Greta, rest, heal. The pain and suffering will all be over soon, and you will have your dream."

What dream?

Gabe looked through the window, saw the last glow of sunset, smiled, and quietly left the room.

Greta awoke to the gentle tones of Chopin... remnants of a lovely dream. She smiled and tried to hold onto the fleeting feeling of love and peace she'd been enjoying in Gabe's arms.

Slowly, awareness reached her mind. She sat straight up and looked around. She wasn't sure what to expect but was somewhat surprised that Gabe wasn't lying in bed next to her.

The way I was blabbering and blubbering last night, he probably took off, and may still be running, she thought.

Greta went to the bathroom, brushed her teeth, and then let the shower ease her aching muscles. She felt almost like new as she headed for the kitchen, when her nose told her she wasn't alone in the house. The aroma of fresh coffee wafted down the hall, and as she got closer, she could hear him rattling around.

"Wow," she said entering the kitchen. "Looks like you've been busy in here," she said trying to push away her embarrassment from yesterday's events.

"Yeah, I hope you don't mind. I crashed on your couch last night. I would have asked, but you were out cold."

"I'm sorry, but you didn't have to stay, you know. I'm fine."

"Sure, I know." He smiled back. "But I was pretty tired, too. Figured I'd show you my chef skills this morning, and then we can pick up where we left off."

"Left off?" she asked incredulously. "I think I told you pretty much my whole life story."

"Well, let me at least finish cooking us up some breakfast, okay? Coffee's ready and I'm just starting the bacon. Can you grab the eggs for me?"

Greta retrieved them, then poured herself some coffee. She sat at the counter watching Gabe cook breakfast, and was amused at how out of place he looked there. He was really quite beautiful.

Funny, she thought *Why 'beautiful' rather than handsome or good-looking?* Strangely, she was drawn to him in a different yet familiar way. As she watched, she was mesmerized by an otherworldly light that surrounded him.

Okay, maybe I need more sleep.

Lost in her thoughts, she didn't realize until he put the plate in front of her that Gabe had finished making their breakfast. It was nice to be taken care of and to have someone to enjoy breakfast with.

Greta put their plates and utensils in the dishwasher when they were done, washed the pans, and refilled their coffee mugs before moving into the sunroom.

She curled up in the big chair she loved, and with her hands wrapped around her warm cup of joe, looked over at Gabe who was watching her intently. She saw something in his eyes she couldn't read, but she felt loved. It was different from anything she'd known before. This was something more. Two words came to mind: *understanding* and *acceptance*, but she didn't know why. At least not yet.

Greta's mind went back to the dark years. She remembered the agony of her life in captivity. She couldn't have been more of a prisoner if there had been a lock on her door and bars on the windows. Sure, she had walked in and out of the house, but she had no choice but to return each day. No choice but to live with the dirty little secret her uncle had thrust upon her. Yet she wondered, *What would have happened if I'd just had the nerve to tell? Maybe I should have run away. But no, I stayed and allowed it to continue for all those years.*

"Greta..."

Though he spoke softly, Greta jumped at the sound. She looked at Gabe with tortured eyes, and he saw her pain.

"Talk to me, Greta. Tell me about it."

"Tell you about what?" she asked. *Was he reading her mind?*

"...about how you're feeling right now, about the anger."

"What anger? I'm... I don't know what you're talking about!" Greta could feel herself getting agitated. "What's your problem, Gabe? What are you after?" she asked in utter frustration.

He crossed the room, and taking her hand, looked into her eyes and said, "Greta, I'm not trying to hurt you. I just want to help. You're beautiful... inside and out... and you've tortured yourself long enough."

"What do you know about it?" she asked harshly. Confused, she could feel herself losing control, but something in his eyes drew her out. With little warning came a flood of words mixed with tears.

"Oh, Gabe, it was so awful! Why? Why did he hurt me like that? He said he loved me... but I begged him not to touch me. I begged him! And I begged God! Why wouldn't He answer my prayers? I... night after night, crying into my pillow and praying but He never answered!"

They had somehow moved to the divan, and Gabe was holding her in his arms as she sobbed in anger and despair.

Running out of steam and energy Greta's sobs subsided before Gabe said, "But it's over. You got away from him. You don't have to be afraid. You're stronger now, Greta, and getting stronger every day. No one will ever hurt you like that again. I promise."

"Are you sure about that?" she choked. "I thought I saw him a couple of times, but when I looked again, he wasn't there. I've been so afraid. I see him when he's not even there," she laughed nervously. "I avoid going anywhere near the neighborhood where they live. I did run into Aunt Kim once. It was after I broke up with this guy I really cared about. I told you about him, right? Tony?"

Gabe nodded.

"Well, one Sunday afternoon, not long after our relationship fell apart, I was feeling really crappy and had to get out of the house to end my pity party, so I went to the mall, just to be around other people, y'know? I was in Nordstrom's basement browsing when all of a sudden I found myself face to face with my aunt. It was kind of funny in a way. She looked as shocked as I felt, and neither of us said anything. I finally asked if she was okay, and how she was doing. She told me she was all right but that Uncle Don wasn't doing so well. She said he was even moodier than he used to be and that he'd lost weight. What, was I supposed to feel sorry for him? I just mumbled something about having to get going and told her to take care of herself then got out of there as quickly as I could. Honest to God, Gabe, I think she blames me. She does. She blames me!"

"Greta, that's her only way of coping. The only way your Aunt Kim can live with herself..."

"Maybe it was my fault... I shouldn't have let him..."

"No!" Gabe raised his voice in anger. "It was *not* your fault. You were a child! My God, think about it. Imagine some little eleven or twelve-year-old girl. Not you, some other little girl. Think about some man she trusts telling her the things your uncle told you. Would you blame that little girl, huh? Would you blame a little girl for the evil being done to her, really?"

In that moment Greta was that little girl again. She hurt like she had so long ago. The pain she had buried was still there. She'd been hiding from it, but now the tears began to wash it away.

Gabe held her tight, whispering, "Let it go, Greta. Let it out, and let it go. The worst is over. You're not a vulnerable little girl anymore. He will never control you again."

Chapter 26

In the days leading up to Thanksgiving, Greta had a recurrent nagging feeling she couldn't quite put her finger on. Something wasn't right. The feeling snuck up on her when she least expected it.

One afternoon leaving the market, she hopped into her car and felt a sudden chill. She looked around nervously, then put the car in gear. *What's wrong with me?* She drove home, fixed dinner and went through her usual evening routines with nothing going awry.

Finally, she pushed the feeling aside. Greta never saw the black pickup that slowly cruised along behind her. She never saw the once familiar driver or the look of madness in his eyes.

Chapter 27

Thanksgiving Day

Greta busied herself making her baked corn casserole. It was something her grandmother had always made for Thanksgiving. It was as much a part of the holiday feast for Greta as the turkey and stuffing.

After the accident, when Greta had gone back to the house, she picked up her Grammy's recipe box. Some of her happiest memories were of Sunday afternoons spent baking with her grandmother so that box meant more to her than any jewelry or money or other valuables from the house. She'd inherited all of it, of course, and had the trust which was set up for her, but above all else, she still cherished the box of pictures on the shelf in her closet, her Grammy's crucifix, and this box of recipes.

So on this festive Thanksgiving morning Greta was warmed by Grammy's Baked Corn recipe. She knew it by heart, but savored holding the well-worn, yellowing card with the beautifully familiar handwriting. She hummed the tunes her Grammy once hummed as they'd worked together in the kitchen. Grammy loved show tunes and would sing, hum, or whistle the songs, read directions aloud for Greta, and go right back to the melody without skipping a beat.

This morning Greta hummed her favorite tunes from *The Sound of Music* as she worked, but without realizing, she slipped into another tune. Chopin. Out of curiosity, Greta had done a search and discovered that the piece was Chopin's *Nocturne in E-Flat Major*. And now, as she hummed, the melody seemed to massage her soul.

Gabe knocked on the door precisely at noon, and Shane moved to the back seat of the car so Greta could sit up front. The trio was in high spirits as they headed to Maria and Freddie's.

The smell of turkey greeted them at the door. After hugs all around, Greta took her casserole to the kitchen. The men followed with their contribution to the festivities. Gabe presented a bottle of Greta's favorite white wine, and Shane brought a nice Merlot. Surrounded by all the wonderful sights and smells of the day's feast, Greta knew there was much to be thankful for in this household. She could see the love Maria and Freddie shared.

This is all I've ever wanted—a wonderful marriage and a beautiful child.

Greta was healing from her broken relationship with Tom... and she had Gabe.

Or did she?

॰•॰

Maria and Greta had a tradition of joining the masses in the craziness of "Black Friday." This would be the fourth year they'd gone out to fight the crowds in search of promised bargains. Together they devoured the store ads after devouring the Thanksgiving feast. Gabe and Freddie were happily enjoying the football games, and the baby was tuckered out and already sleeping, so the girls planned their strategy for the next morning's adventure.

They made an early evening of it with Gabe and Shane heading home. Greta slept over because Black Friday meant getting up early to hit the malls and capture their prizes.

Before the sun peeked over the horizon, the girls were out of bed and jumping into their clothes. Their first stop was the toy store, of course. When it came right down to it, that's what this trip was all about. There was nothing more fun than shopping for little Ariana. Greta was the child's godmother and absolutely adored the toddler. She dreamed of the day she would have children of her own, but in the meantime she poured all that love on Maria's little one.

They found a really good buy on an adorable big stuffed animal they knew she'd love. It was a purple unicorn with a pink mane, and Greta could already picture Ariana hugging and loving it to pieces. They also got her two hand puppets, some building blocks, a couple of toddler puzzles, and a life-like baby doll in a lavender outfit (Ariana's favorite color). They even got her a little stroller to walk her baby. But their biggest bargain of the day was the little pink car she could drive all around the house.

"I know her eyes are gonna light up when she sees this!" Maria said, and Greta warmed at the thought.

By the time the girls finished shopping for Ariana, they had worked up an appetite and headed for the food-court. Between bites Maria asked, "So you're doing okay now, huh? I mean a lot better than you were... you know, after Tom walked out."

"Yeah, I am," Greta answered thoughtfully. "I'm not sure where this thing with Gabe is going, but I really like him, and he's been, I don't know... like really good medicine!" she laughed as she finished.

"Good! He's good people. Different... but honestly, I trust him."

"What do you mean, you trust him?" Greta smiled back at her friend. "You're not seeing him on the side are you?" she winked.

"No, smart-ass," Maria laughed. "I mean I trust him for you. I don't think he'll hurt you. I worry about you, ya know, girlfriend."

Maria had seen Greta hurt more than once, and she also knew enough history to know Greta had endured more pain in her life than anyone deserved.

"Maria, I think you're right. Gabe would never do anything to hurt me, at least not intentionally."

"So what about Shane?" Maria asked.

Confused, Greta responded, "What do you mean? He's just a friend of Gabe's."

Maria's smile held a secret question as she added, "...a very good-looking friend, I'd say."

Greta laughed. "Okay, so enough gabbing. We're on a mission here. You're done, right?"

"Yep! *Vámonos!*"

The subject of Shane was dropped, but thoughts of him lingered.

Having finished with the toy purchases, they headed up the mall to pick out gifts for other family, friends, and coworkers.

"I want to stop at the music store before we call it a day, okay?" Greta said.

When they got there Greta headed right for the classical section.

"Whoa? Really?" Maria laughed. "I know you're shopping for somebody else now!"

"Hey! Not so fast! You don't know. Maybe I'm getting some culture on the sly." Greta attempted an uppity expression. "Actually, I'll have you know I have discovered that some classical music ain't half bad!" She laughed again, saying, "But you're right. I'm looking for something for Gabe."

"Aha! So that's where your new appreciation of the arts is coming from."

Maria enjoyed teasing her friend and Greta enjoyed the fact that she was doing well enough to be teased.

Greta settled on a collection of great masterpieces to go with the sweater she'd purchased for him earlier. She didn't want to get carried away and 'over-gift' him as was her habit. *Shower them with gifts... make them happy so they won't leave...* but not this time. This time it was just because.

Chapter 28

In the days and weeks after the storm, Greta discovered she was more relaxed with Gabe. They saw each other nearly every day, met for lunch or dinner, and spent most evenings at the house. They spent weekends together taking in the sights around Baltimore, traveling to Annapolis and Washington, and enjoying each other's company wherever they were. Occasionally, they made it a trio, including Shane in their jaunts. The three laughed together like old friends, and Greta found that she looked forward to the times Shane would join them.

Greta was puzzled that Gabe didn't pursue a more intimate relationship. She knew he cared more about her well-being than anyone, and when she was with him, she felt safe, warm, loved and protected. Like she had when Grammy was alive.

He held her hand, put his arm around her, and ended evenings with a warm hug and a kiss on the cheek. It was more fatherly than anything. Perhaps even more puzzling, Greta didn't mind.

Even though they didn't share her bed, Greta knew she loved him. But she didn't *need* him.

About three weeks after their stormy boat ride and the stormier revelations, they were enjoying a lazy Sunday.

"Hey, how would you like to help me pick out a Christmas tree?" Greta asked.

"Sure, why not?" Gabe replied with a big grin. He started to get up but seemed to lose his balance and fell back into the chair.

"What's wrong?" Greta rushed to his side. "What is it, Gabe? Are you okay?" she asked. Taking his hand, concern covered her face.

He sat very still for a minute then got up slowly. "...Just a little dizzy," he smiled. "Maybe on the way to get that tree we'd better grab some lunch."

"Sounds like a plan!" Greta laughed but couldn't shrug off her concern.

☙❧

After grabbing a quick burger, then checking out just about every tree on the lot, Greta was confident the one they brought home was the best. Of course when they got it back to the house, it had a bit of a bare spot on one side.

They made the necessary adjustments and stood back to admire their tree. Greta was excited about Christmas, more excited than she remembered being in a very long time. Last Christmas things were already falling apart with Tom, and they went through the motions without the real joy of the season.

"Gabe, what would you like for Christmas?" Greta smiled.

"Well now, I'm going to have to give that a little thought. Let's see... a Mercedes maybe? Or how about a big house with a pool, and oh yeah, throw in a few servants?" He chuckled with this last request, and Greta liked the sound of his laugh. It was so easy and genuine.

"Yeah, well I think you'd better ask one of Santa's other helpers for those gifts!" she laughed at him. "I was thinking more along the lines of the usual ugly tie." She winked.

With that special twinkle she only ever saw in Gabe, he spoke more earnestly. "Greta, the only gift I really want this year is to see the pain gone from your eyes."

"I'm not sure what special super powers you have that let you see whatever it is you think you're seeing," she said sarcastically, "but you might just have to settle for the tie!"

Now he laughed outright, "An ugly tie will be just fine."

Greta was grateful to be enjoying the season she had dreaded only months before.

Gabe left a little later, kissing her lightly on the cheek. *Gabe Engel, who are you, anyway?* she wondered.

Two days later Gabe returned to help decorate the tree. With Christmas carols playing softly, they worked together trimming and singing until the tree was beautifully adorned. Then Greta reached for a tattered old shoe box on the floor.

"What's that?" Gabe asked. She smiled as she gently opened the lid and turned back the protective tissue paper.

"This is the angel Grammy and I picked out and put on our tree…" Greta paused to choke back unexpected tears. "It sat on the top of our tree… on the last Christmas we had together." Through tears she looked up at Gabe who was suddenly by her side. He wrapped her in his arms and kissed the top of her head. "Would you put it up for me?" she whispered.

"I would be honored."

With the final ornament on the tree, they sat in the dark, sipping hot chocolate, and admiring the result. It really did look quite beautiful. *This feels so right.*

Greta's mind wandered. She thought of Shane and was about to ask if he could join them on Christmas day when Gabe stood up to go to the bathroom and lost his balance. He braced himself against the wall.

Alarmed, Greta asked "What's wrong, Gabe?"

He took a moment to regain his equilibrium, then smiled. "It was nothing. I guess I just got up too fast."

All thoughts of Shane flew out of her mind.

While Gabe was in the bathroom, Greta remembered times the same thing had happened to her, but when he returned, she noticed his lack of color. She was also pretty sure he'd lost weight in the short time she'd known him.

"What?" he asked. "You're staring, you know." Greta shared her concerns, but Gabe reassured her, "Yeah, I think I've lost about ten pounds, but that's because I needed to. Got to watch out not to get that middle-age spread, you know?" His boyish grin belied the idea he was anywhere near the age of worrying about that. "But I am kind of tired. It's been a long, busy day. I should probably get home so I can get a good night's sleep. Work day mornings have a way of coming so early!"

Gabe hadn't spent the night, albeit on the sofa, since the weekend of their fateful boat ride. Greta wondered now if he ever would.

They said goodnight with Gabe reassuring her again that he was fine, and she closed the door behind him, only then remembering she hadn't asked about Shane. When she headed to bed a short time later, a nagging worry followed her into her dreams.

The orchestra was playing a familiar tune as Greta and Gabe circled the dance floor. Greta felt comfortable, safe, and happy as they moved to the soothing sound of Chopin once more. She looked up into his eyes and saw the love reflected there... but the face, it wasn't Gabe... It was her father... those same eyes looked into hers. Softly he said, "I'm so sorry I have to go." It wasn't her father now; it was Gabe, and she felt the panic building. "No, you can't go! Don't leave me... please, no... Don't go!" She was crying, she was alone and the music ended. It was dark, and she was frightened.

Greta woke with a start, the silence of her dream jolted by the alarm clock's wail. She sat trembling in the memory and felt lost.

Greta called Gabe later during her lunch break. She needed to hear his voice. Gabe sounded fine, of course. They met for a quick supper, and she was struck again by the special quality in his eyes. There was that kind of twinkle and there was love. *His eyes*, she thought, *are so full of love, and so familiar.*

"Hey, wake up, lady," Gabe said with amusement. "Come back from wherever you were before the waitress comes for your order. You haven't even opened your menu."

"Oh sorry... Good idea," she smiled in agreement.

By the time they parted Greta had put her concerns aside, convinced that she was just a worrier and needed to relax. But still she couldn't shake that sense of dread.

Chapter 29

December 23

Greta enjoyed the sounds, sights and smells of the season. There were the occasional moments of nostalgia remembering Christmas preparations with Grammy, but she remembered them with more fondness than pain.

Then there were the Christmases spent with her aunt and uncle, filled with presents and cookies and all the usual trimmings, but none of the joy.

During her time with Tony, Christmas had been a delight—at least parts of it—and she and Terry had a great time celebrating before she'd tried to get too serious. She realized now that their time together had lacked something, but back then it had seemed to be all that holidays should be.

Then there was her Christmas with Tom. She'd tried to make it perfect, as was her habit, but again missed the mark.

Ah Greta, you and your poor choices, she laughed to herself. *No more men with the first initial T.* Her musings continued as she browsed the little shops at the harbor looking for last-minute gifts and decorations.

An hour before, Greta had been at the office holiday party. She liked her co-workers, but wasn't particularly close with any except her secretary. Her duties these days didn't involve working directly with other people so much as pushing papers, video and phone conferences, and countless emails. There wasn't much time for face-to-face conversations with anyone during her workday.

"Greta!" She turned to see her secretary, Kathy, walking toward her. "I finished those orders and faxed them over so everything's caught up."

"Kathy, you're a gem. Thank you, and Merry Christmas." She gave her a warm hug. "I'm ready for a few days off. Are you all set for your visit with your folks?" Greta was finally comfortable talking with someone she knew and cared about. They exchanged a few more pleasantries, then she noticed Kathy's repeated glances across the room. Following her gaze, she saw a very good-looking young man glancing back at her secretary.

"So who's that handsome guy? He's obviously interested." She saw the color rush to Kathy's cheeks as she looked down at the floor. When she looked up again, her smile said it all.

"That's Doug. He just started in customer service."

"Well, he's obviously anxious to talk to you. Go!" Greta laughed. Kathy thanked her and was gone. Greta felt alone in the crowded room again.

I've got to get out of here. I don't even know half of these people.

She slowly made her way to the door wishing Merry Christmas to friends and strangers on her way. Some people were already drinking too much, and she didn't feel like watching them make fools of themselves. Greta had seen enough of how alcohol could affect human behavior watching Uncle Don.

So by three o'clock she was out of there and enjoying the time to relax and soak in the joyous feel of the holiday. She couldn't remember looking forward to Christmas day with this much enthusiasm in a very long time.

Greta thought about Ariana. She knew the toddler would be an absolute hoot this year, and she was going to be there to enjoy watching her open presents. Maria and Freddie insisted Greta spend the night with them Christmas Eve. They wouldn't hear of her waking up alone on Christmas morning.

So the plan was for Greta and Gabe to go to dinner in Little Italy, just the two of them, then they'd meet up with the Garcia family for midnight mass. After mass, Gabe would drive Greta back to Maria's, and rejoin them around noon on Christmas Day. He was invited to stay over with them but had graciously declined.

Greta thought of Shane and was glad they had also invited him to join them.

"Sorry. People still need care on Christmas day," Shane told them. "Unfortunately, we often have a lot of action in the ER on most holidays, including Christmas."

Such is the life of a doctor, Greta supposed.

Totally lost in thought, she didn't see the man in front of her until she ran right smack into him.

"Oh, I'm so sorry, I...." she stopped mid-sentence, staring into a face she'd hoped never to see again. Greta backed up reflexively, and looked into his menacing eyes. He looked so much older than she remembered... like many more years had passed than in actuality.

"How are you, Greta?" he asked as if nothing horrible and ugly had ever happened between them. The old familiar smell of alcohol assaulted her nose.

"I'm great, actually," she said with bravado she didn't feel. "How are Aunt Kim and Bobby?" She could hear the quiver in her voice and hated that this man could affect her like that. All she could think was that she needed to get away from him. He obviously couldn't do anything to hurt her... not here in this public place, anyway.

"They're okay. Greta, I've missed you. You know, it would be all right if you wanted to come see me... I mean, us, sometime. No hard feelings."

Greta stared at him in utter disbelief. She couldn't believe her ears. Was he really inviting her back into that house? She was stunned.

"Tell Aunt Kim and Bobby I said Merry Christmas. I've got to get going." She heard her own words and knew how inane they sounded as she turned and rushed away from him.

"Greta," she heard him call after her, and quickened her step, afraid to look back.

Shaken to the core, it was only after she'd run down the escalator and was making her way to the parking garage that the tears began to flow.

☙❧

Greta was suddenly desperate to talk to Gabe. Once home, she turned off the engine and grabbed her cell. He answered on the first ring with a festive greeting. The only response was a sob.

"Greta, what's wrong?"

"Can you come over?" Greta could feel her cheeks and ears burning.

"Of course... I can be there in about fifteen minutes." He was there in ten. He found her still sitting in the car. Opening the driver's side door, he pulled her into his arms then guided her into the house.

"Everything's going to be okay. Just sit, take your time. We'll talk when you're ready." Gabe settled her on the couch. "I can make us some coffee, or get you a soda or glass of wine? Better yet, maybe water?"

Greta nodded. *He always knows what I really need.*

Gabe pushed a glass against the ice dispenser on the fridge, filled it with water, and placed it in Greta's trembling hands. She let it wash the cotton out of her mouth before trying to speak. Gabe put his arm around her shoulders and waited. Greta took a breath.

"I saw him today, my uncle... I ran into him at the harbor." The words came faster. "I didn't see him, and all of a sudden there he was. I was staring into his face." She looked up at Gabe for help.

"You're okay, now. It's okay. You're safe now, Greta."

"It was awful! I didn't know what to say. He... he acted like he was just some long lost relative... Asked me how I was doing." Greta jumped to her feet and began pacing. "Oh God, I was so scared! I just had to get away from him. What is wrong with him? How can he act like nothing happened?"

Then Gabe was by her side. He took her by the shoulders and looked straight into her eyes.

"He's a sick man. We don't always know what makes people turn out the way they do, but you can bet someone must have hurt him real bad. You've heard that saying, hurt people hurt people? Well, it's true." He pulled her close. "Some people have the will and determination to do whatever it takes to heal. Some don't. The bitterness of their wounds festers until the hate eats them alive."

Then lifting her chin he looked at her intensely and added, "But Greta, he can't hurt you anymore. You're not a little girl. You're not powerless. You will never let him hurt you again."

Greta hadn't moved. She was sobbing, but she heard Gabe's words and somehow knew it was true. She would never let *that man* hurt her again. She used the tissues Gabe handed her, and pulled herself together with new resolve.

"You must think I'm a mess," she said.

"No, I think you've been hurt... and hurt badly, and it takes a while to heal."

"Gabe?" He looked up. "I'm going to be okay."

He smiled. "I know."

⁂

Don Taylor sat in the green Ford Explorer parked across the street and two doors up. He hadn't been able to catch up to Greta without being noticed and lost her in the Christmas crowds.

But he knew where she lived.

At the sight of her boyfriend's car parked in front, rage burned from his stomach up to his throat.

"You won't be able to hide behind your new boyfriend forever, you ungrateful little slut." Don threw the car into drive. "Our time will come. I'm a patient man."

Chapter 30

Christmas Day

"Auntie Gweta, look... look at all the pwesents."

Greta woke up laughing. Ariana's nose was right in front of her as the little girl patted her cheek. She opened her eyes wide with excitement.

"Oh wow, Ariana! Looks like Santa was here while we were sleeping!"

"Yeah!" Ariana shouted and ran to the tree. "Mama, can we open the pwesents now? Pwease, can we open them?"

Maria walked in carrying two coffee mugs. She handed one to Greta. Freddie was right behind her, and they both had sleepy eyes and big smiles.

"Are you ready for this, girlfriend?" Maria asked.

Greta curled up on the end of the couch and pulled the blanket up around her. "Absolutely!"

Freddie sat on the other end of the couch while his wife took a spot on the floor next to her little girl who was now jumping up and down with excitement.

Maria hugged Ariana and handed her the first gift to open. Snuggled up with her coffee, Greta watched the fun-filled chaos.

And someday, she thought, *they can come and share the joy with me and my husband and children.* For the first time in years, Greta believed this really could be a part of her future.

Ariana giggled with delight at each new present. It was amazing how much she'd grown since last Christmas and how much more excited she was. The magic of the season was here in this room.

When Ariana ripped the wrapping off her final present, her daddy found a note from Santa. "It says there's one more present for Ariana that wouldn't fit under the tree."

The child's eyes grew wide, and she started running around excitedly. "Where is it? Where did Santa put it?"

"Well, it says here that you should look in the garage."

Ariana was at the garage door well ahead of her daddy, pulling at the handle.

Freddie laughed with the happy sound of a father who knew the gift of such a child. "Hold up now, mira, let me see what I can find." He stepped out into the garage and reappeared in seconds carrying in the Little Tikes Cozy Coupe.

"It's a car!" Ariana squealed. "It's my car." She jumped up and down and ran round and round her car while the adults all shared in her joy.

A little while later, with Ariana somewhat calmer and entertaining herself with all her new toys, the adults exchanged gifts. They were very generous with each other and the love they felt showed in their choices.

Afterward, Freddie said to Greta, "Maria did give me one gift last night that I want to show you."

He handed her a little box in which she found a note. On it was written:

Papa, we are going to give Ariana a little brother or sister.
I love you so much!
Maria

Somehow in the next moment Greta was hugging both her friends, and they all cried tears of joy.

Distracted by the grown-ups' odd behavior, Ariana asked, "What's wrong, Mama?"

Maria laughed through her tears. "Nothing, my sweet baby. Nothing is wrong. Everything is good. Life is good. God is good!"

Ariana watched for a moment, and, deciding the crazy grown-ups must be okay, went back to her toys.

Once the three of them settled down from the excitement of sharing Maria's news, they had a late breakfast.

"We always have French toast on Christmas morning. Does that work for you, girlfriend?" Maria asked.

"Yum... you betcha! Can I help?" Greta asked.

"Oh no, the best part of this tradition is that Freddie's the chef." Maria winked and poured them all another coffee. Her husband obviously knew his way around the kitchen.

"Who knew a *Latino* could make such amazing French toast?" Greta laughed as she reached for another slice. "This one is definitely a keeper, Maria."

Freddie laughed and told his wife not to forget it.

"Hey, don't let it go to your head, man."

The breakfast was delicious, but being part of this family—even if only for a while—was what she loved most. She ached to have what her friends had.

This is all I've ever wanted. Maybe someday...

☙❧

Gabe arrived around two o'clock, and Greta realized how glad she was to see him. She had a right to have someone too, and Gabe was the best man she'd ever known.

She met him with an enthusiastic hug, and after he'd been given a drink and cookies, Greta got his gifts from under the tree where she'd placed them the night before.

"Ariana, let's show Daddy your purple unicorn. Maybe you can give it a ride in your new car."

With a quick glance at Greta and a wink over her shoulder, Maria took Freddie by the hand and followed their giggling toddler into the playroom. Greta and Gabe would be alone, at least for a little while.

Gabe smiled warmly and opened his first gift. Greta was relieved to see the big smile on his face when he saw the CD she'd gotten for him.

"Ah, this was a perfect choice, Greta. So thoughtful, thank you."

The genuineness of his words warmed her heart. He said he really liked the sweater she'd gotten him as well, and the color was perfect on him. The burgundy somehow made his eyes look even bluer.

Then it was his turn to give Greta her gift. She tore open the paper on a package that was a similar size to the one she'd given him, and found that it was also a CD. The title was, "Classical Music for People Who Hate Classical Music."

"Absolutely perfect!" she laughed with him. "And I've discovered that I don't so much hate classical music after all. Well, okay, some of it is a little much for me..."

Gabe laughed too, agreeing.

Greta looked at the disc again, reading over the titles of the selections, and yes, it was there... *Nocturne in E-Flat Major*. She smiled knowing that was why he'd picked it. It reminded her of the dream.

When she opened the second gift, her jaw dropped, and she looked up at Gabe in surprise.

"How did you know?"

"Do you remember the night of the storm..."

"Are you kidding?" Greta asked. "How could I forget it? But what's that got to do with a sketchpad?"

"If you'll recall, you were so exhausted I walked you into the bedroom, and you were asleep in seconds."

"Yes, I remember."

"Well, I noticed a sketchpad on your bedside table and I took a look inside. You're really good by the way... and I loved the pictures of the little girl." Greta looked down at the floor, slightly embarrassed and thanked him shyly. She wondered if she should be annoyed that his prying eyes had seen her most precious drawings... but for some reason she wasn't.

"Anyway, I figured since it was almost full, you might be needing a new one soon."

"You were right," she said stroking the tablet. "and I really appreciate it." Gabe always seemed to know what she needed. "So, have you talked to Shane today? I mean, did you get a chance to wish him a Merry Christmas?" Unsure why Shane had just popped into her thoughts, she felt an unexplained sense of guilt.

"Yes," Gabe answered, "he wasn't available when I first telephoned but he returned my call a bit later. We didn't talk long... sounded like he was pretty busy."

"Well, I'm sorry he couldn't spend the day with us, but I understand he's needed there."

Later in the day, Maria and Greta set about getting their Christmas meal together while the men relaxed in the den. Ariana napped, exhausted from the excitement of the morning. As soon as she awoke, they were ready to sit down to a dinner of baked ham, pineapple, homemade potato salad, green bean casserole, rolls and butter. There was apple pie and ice cream for dessert with lots of Christmas cookies and fudge besides.

They retired to the living room with an after-dinner cordial, full tummies, and complete satisfaction. Ariana's adorable antics entertained four tired but happy grownups, but after a few minutes, Greta noticed Gabe hadn't had much to say since dinner.

"Are you all right, Gabe?" she asked with concern.

"I'm fine. Just tired. We've been going non-stop the last few days." He laughed and added, "I guess I'm getting old... but I'm fine." Greta wasn't so sure. Concern gnawed at her for the rest of the evening though she tried to let it go and accept his explanation.

By early evening, Greta noticed Gabe was looking strained and rather pale. She decided it was time to call it a night and asked if he wanted to come over to the house for a while.

He smiled. "I'm never too tired to spend time with the people I care about. How 'bout if I follow you over?"

When they arrived at her house, Greta offered him something to drink. He declined, saying he would only be staying for a little while. They settled onto the couch, and Greta looked at him closely.

"Gabe, please tell me the truth. Are you really all right?"

"Well, I guess I've been better." He smiled and added, "I don't seem to have much energy lately, and I do feel like I'm about 110 years old."

"Have you considered calling a doctor? I'm worried about you. Your color isn't too good, you're tired, and how about those dizzy spells? Something is going on. You really should get it checked."

"Yes, mother," he winked.

"Do you have a doctor here in Baltimore?"

"As a matter of fact I know one particular doctor very well, and I don't think I'll have any trouble getting an appointment with him," he said with a knowing smile. "It's Shane."

"Oh, of course!"

"Yeah, pretty handy, huh, having a close friend who's also your doctor?"

"Great, so you'll call him?"

"Yes, Greta, I'll call him tomorrow. I promise. He's working at the hospital so I know where to find him, okay?" He patted her hand and stood to leave, but halfway to the door he staggered. Gabe grabbed for the doorknob and then collapsed.

"Gabe, Gabe, oh my God, are you okay?" He didn't respond. Greta fell to her knees by his side and put her head on his chest. Relieved to feel him breathing, she grabbed frantically for her phone, and dialed 911.

The minutes waiting for help seemed like forever. Greta held his wrist feeling his pulse for reassurance. She spoke softly trying to ward off the panic crawling up her spine.

"Come on, Gabe. Wake up. You're going to be fine. You... you've got to be fine." She saw his lids flutter. "Gabe, Gabe, can you hear me? You're going to be okay. I called for help..."

The sirens blared just as Gabe slowly regained consciousness. He looked up at Greta and the EMTs who rushed to his side.

"I'm okay. I'll be all right in a minute. Just got dizzy."

"Take it easy, sir. Let us just check your vitals."

Greta hovered while giving them room to work. The female EMT looked at Greta and nodded reassuringly.

"Okay, Gabe," the other one said. "Your blood pressure is still pretty low, so we're just gonna take you over to the hospital and let them keep you under observation and do a more thorough examination, okay?"

Gabe started to object, but seeing the worry on Greta's face, finally agreed.

Greta knew he'd only agreed to put her mind at rest.

She insisted on going to be with him and waited anxiously for the results of his exam. Finally she saw the white coat she'd been watching for.

"Is he all right, Shane?"

"Yes, we're discharging him now. He's fine to go home, but I scheduled a follow-up appointment so we can run some tests... just to be safe."

Since she had followed the ambulance with her car, Greta drove Gabe home. She would have felt better if he'd agreed to come back to her house, but he wouldn't hear it.

"Now, stop worrying, Greta. I'll feel better when I get home and get a good night's sleep in my own bed. Trust me, okay?"

When she pulled up in front of his place, Greta looked at him and was somewhat satisfied since he'd been checked out by Shane. His color had even improved.

Gabe smiled sheepishly back at her. "I'm sorry I messed up your Christmas, Greta."

"What?" Greta asked, incredulously. "Are you kidding me? This was the best Christmas I can remember since I was a little kid!"

He laughed.

"No, really," she said. "This has been a wonderful day. Sure, you tried to put a damper on it at the very end, but since Shane said you're okay, it's all good."

The smile on her face seemed to reassure Gabe.

He gently stroked her cheek and said, "My sweet Greta, your Christmases are going to get better and better, I promise." Then with a tender kiss on her cheek, he said good-night.

As Greta headed home, she wondered if he could be right. It all seemed too good to be true.

Could I actually get my happily ever after? Is that even possible?

Chapter 31

The day after Christmas was usually a bit of a letdown for Greta. The excitement and anticipation never quite measured up to the reality of the day. That is, until this year.

Greta curled up in her favorite spot on the couch, sipping cinnamon streusel coffee and looking at her tree. She found herself savoring the memories of an almost perfect day. One of the highlights, of course, was Maria's 'gift' to Freddie. Greta was almost as excited as the parents-to-be.

And Ariana was such a joy to watch when they finally told her the news. Her parents explained that she was going to be a big sister and they were going to have a real baby for her to help take care of.

"And you can practice with your new baby doll," Maria had told her.

Greta wondered if Maria already had that in mind when they'd picked out the doll and stroller together.

The day had gotten even better, of course, when Gabe got there. He made her feel so valued, so cherished. Greta was amazed at how much better she felt about herself... about everything since he had come into her life.

The CD he'd given her was playing, and Greta was surprised by how familiar some of the melodies were. She recognized movie themes, music from cartoons, and most familiar of all... the beautiful notes of Chopin that had carried her and dream-Gabe across the dance floor. On impulse Greta opened her new sketchpad, grabbed her pencil, and began to draw the dancers.

The phone interrupted her work. She answered quickly and with some concern when she saw Gabe's caller ID. After all, it wasn't too many hours ago that he'd fallen to the floor in this very room.

"Good morning, sunshine," he said cheerfully. "How are you this beautiful day?"

Greta let her breath out. He sounded okay. "I'm just fine, my friend. How about you? Seems to me you're the one we need to worry about."

"Don't worry, Greta. I'm feeling better, and I already called Shane this morning. He's going to see me tomorrow afternoon to run tests and whatever else a good physician does."

"Thank you! You men just hate to go see your doctors, I know, but it's good to get a thorough check-up to be on the safe side."

"Yeah, yeah, okay. Enough about that. Do you have lunch plans?" he asked.

"Nope, what do you have in mind?"

"Well, when I called Shane, we were talking, and he mentioned how much he enjoyed Thanksgiving with us. Since he had to work through Christmas, I was thinking maybe we could all go to lunch together. We could call the Garcias and invite them along too, if you'd like."

"That sounds like fun, sure! I'll give Maria a call."

Promising to get back to him as soon as she checked with her BFF, she hung up. Gabe made her happy. He was like a warm comfortable blanket. She couldn't imagine life without him.

Yet she couldn't deny the excitement as she anticipated seeing Shane again.

☙❧

"Oh my goodness... my face hurts from laughing so hard!" Maria pushed her dessert plate away. "Eating and laughing that hard is takin' a toll on this pregnant lady."

Freddie put his arm around his wife and looked across the table at Shane. "Now look what you've done!" he said accusingly.

It was true. At everyone's urging Shane had shared one crazy anecdote after another about the hospital.

"My apologies," Shane bowed his head in feigned remorse, initiating even more laughter.

Lunch was definitely a success. And by the end of their two hours together, Shane had become part of their little family.

Greta couldn't help comparing Gabe and Shane from time to time. They were alike in so many ways. The genuine laugh, the light in their eyes, even their physical appearance was similar. Shane's hair was a little darker but still blondish, and his eyes were the blue of the sky on a clear day and quite striking. Also they were both nearly six feet tall.

Yes, Greta thought, *both good looking guys.* They were such a contrast to Freddie with his almost black Latin hair and brown eyes. But one thing they all had in common was their sense of humor. *Joie de vivre*, she thought. She wanted that.

But even as she savored the moment, she knew it wasn't that simple. Not for her.

Stop dreaming, girl... she sighed as she glanced in the rearview mirror.

Chapter 32

"All good things must come to an end, but we should do this again," Maria said. "How about New Year's Eve?" she laughed. "It won't be a wild and crazy party, but I think it will be fun."

Gabe and Greta agreed and looked at Shane who also nodded agreement.

"Oh, and would you like to bring someone, Shane?"

"No, I'm not really seeing anyone right now." He glanced self-consciously in Greta's direction and quickly looked away.

Greta's face flushed. She felt relieved that no one else seemed to notice. Then Maria gave her a strange inquiring look.

"No problem," she quickly intervened. "I can set you up with a really cute girl. Dark hair and eyes, kind of short, but she's gorgeous and quite a charmer. Her name's Ariana and I know she's available."

Greta let out her breath as everyone erupted into laughter.

Gabe and Greta said goodbye to the gang out in the parking lot. Shane had a patient he needed to check on back at the hospital. He gave Greta a warm, friendly hug, reminded Gabe not to forget his appointment time, and was gone.

"So Greta, what are you doing for the rest of the day? Do you have plans? Do you want to do something?" Gabe asked when they reached her car.

"I... um," Greta hesitated, then lifted her head, threw back her shoulders, and took a deep breath. "You know what...? I have something I should really take care of, but I might need to see you... or at least talk to you afterward."

"Sure," he replied with concern. "Just call me when you're done, okay? Even if you don't need to, do it for me. Promise?"

Greta let out her breath and smiled up into those blue eyes that always reassured. She agreed.

"Knowing you'll be there makes this a little easier. Thanks, Gabe."

He wrapped her in his arms for several long seconds, and as he released her, she suddenly thought of Shane.

"I'll call you, okay?" she said while her mind raced.

What is wrong with me? But all thoughts of Shane faded when she got back in her car and headed across town.

☙❧

Greta knew exactly where she was going but had no idea what she would do or say when she got there. She drove as though possessed. When she pulled into the driveway of the house she hadn't been to since her senior year in high school, she froze... thoughts racing... *What the hell was I thinking?* She put the car in reverse.

"No," she said aloud, "I've got to do this. I *want* to do this. Damn you, Don Taylor!"

Greta threw the car into park, turned off the engine and jumped out. She headed up the walk. *You can do this, Greta,* she thought. She reached to ring the bell but there was no need. The front door swung open. Aunt Kim had heard the car pull into the driveway and stood stunned to see Greta on her threshold.

"Greta, what are you doing here?" she whispered glancing behind her.

"Where is he, Aunt Kim?"

Greta's timid aunt looked as though she might jump out of her skin.

Quietly she answered, "He's in the den, but..."

Greta walked straight through the house to find him slouched in his usual spot in front of the TV.

"What do you want?" he asked antagonistically, thinking his wife had entered the room.

"I want to talk to you."

Don Taylor spun around wide-eyed at the sound of his niece's voice. The smile that was more of a sneer disappeared when he saw the expression on her face. He paled and slowly came to his feet.

"Greta, it's good to see you. You look upset. Has something happened? Are you all right?"

"No! No, I'm not all right, but I will be."

"Wh...what do you—"

"How can you ask me if I'm all right?" she interrupted. "You made sure I wasn't! You hurt me, Uncle Don!"

"No... I just—"

"Don't interrupt me," Greta said with more bravado than she felt. "I came here to tell you something, and you're going to listen." She could hardly believe the strength she heard in her own voice, and the look on Taylor's face showed his shock.

"What you did was wrong! You said you loved me. Do you even know the meaning of the word?" Her voice went higher and she felt her heart pounding in her chest. "No, that's not really a question. I already know the answer to that. You don't have a clue. All you've ever cared about is yourself."

"Now you just wait a minute..."

"*No!* I will not wait a minute! You're a bully and a child molester," she shouted.

A look of fear came into his eyes. Don Taylor glanced toward the door.

"Are you afraid, Uncle Don? It doesn't feel very good to be afraid, does it?" She felt the rage burning her neck and cheeks. "I know all about that feeling. Yeah, and so does Aunt Kim. Well, it's over. I'm done being afraid of you."

"But Greta, you don't have to be afraid of me. I..."

"Don't! Don't talk to me! I just had to get this off my chest. I know what you did was wrong, and I don't ever want to see you or talk to you again. If you see me somewhere, don't come over to me. Don't talk to me. Don't even look at me. Cross the street to the other side, walk away... better yet, run. I don't care. Just. Stay. Out. Of. My. Life."

Greta turned to leave.

"Greta?" he implored.

"*No!*" she screamed. "If you want to talk to somebody, talk to your wife. Start by apologizing to her for treating her like dirt for all these years. I know that's not likely, but you should think about it. Maybe *she'll* forgive you. Because I can't. I won't!"

Greta turned again and walked quickly out of the house of nightmares. She barely saw her aunt standing near the door as she brushed by, but then paused, turned back to look at her, and said, "You deserve better."

She was glad to feel the cold, fresh air as she left the pain behind. Back in the car, she started the engine, and backed out of the driveway. Glancing around, she saw her aunt still standing at the front door. Then she saw a curtain in the study window move. Greta held it together until she was several blocks away.

☙❧

"Hey, Sunshine. How goes it?"

"Not great." Greta's voice cracked as she swiped at the tears with the back of her hand.

"Are you at home?"

"Not yet. But I'm heading straight there. Can you meet me?"

"Silly question. Greta, are you sure you're okay to drive?"

"Yes, Gabe. Honestly, I'm fine now. But I do want to see you."

"You got it. I'm on my way. And Greta?" he paused. "Never mind, see you shortly."

Chapter 33

Kim Taylor sat holding the phone in one hand and an ice pack in the other. Crouched on the floor by the bed, she listened until she was sure he wasn't coming back. It was only eight-thirty, but her husband's drinking had escalated after Greta's dramatic departure.

She knew he had no business behind the wheel of a car yet she felt nothing but relief when the front door slammed behind him. The roar of the Mustang's engine unlocked her paralysis.

Kim entered her cell phone password and saw Bobby's name at the top of her recent calls. She only hesitated for a moment, then tapped to call. She wouldn't use video tonight. "I can't let him see me like this," she muttered.

"Hiya, Mom. What's up?"

She was filled with relief at hearing her son's familiar greeting. "Are you at home?"

"What did he do?"

She heard fear and anger in Bobby's voice. His accusation filled her with shame. "C...can I come over?"

"I'll come get you."

Kim reflexively touched the side of her face. "No, really, I'm fine. I'll see you in about thirty minutes."

Hanging up the phone she hoped the ice pack had done its job. Bobby's temper was nearly as bad as his father's, and she was afraid of what he might do. *No,* she thought, *I won't be the cause of a fight that could end badly. I'm not going to let your father hurt you, Bobby. He's hurt enough people already.*

Kim Taylor stumbled into the bathroom and threw up, then grabbed her makeup and did her best to cover up the damage on her face. She pitied the woman in the mirror.

Chapter 34

Ever since New Year's Eve at Maria's, Greta felt herself more and more drawn to Shane. She remembered how they'd counted down to midnight. She stood between the two men in her life. All eyes on the TV as the ball dropped. Five... four... three... two... one. Gabe put his hands on her shoulders and placed a gentle kiss on her lips. Greta warmed at the love she saw in his eyes. Then she turned to Shane. He lifted her chin and with a gentle brush of his lips on hers, sent a shock of electricity burning through her.

"Happy New Year, Greta." Barely a whisper...

"H-happy New Year, Shane," Greta laughed nervously. *Did he feel it too?* When he kissed her, it was different from anything she'd felt with Gabe. She tried to push the sensation aside, ashamed, but it had happened. She looked into Shane's eyes and knew he felt something too.

Maria caught her in the kitchen a little later. "Hey girl, is there something going on between you and the good doctor?"

"Don't be silly!" Greta scoffed. "I hardly know him!"

But I'd like to know him better. Greta chided herself for even thinking it. She was with Gabe. *Or am I?* she wondered.

So much had happened in such a short time. Wasn't it just October when Tom had walked out the door and she'd thought her world was ending? Then Gabe walked into her life... and now Shane? *I can't help it if he's gorgeous. And a woman has needs.*

Greta wondered how so much could happen in such a short time. She felt like a different person. She had no idea where life was taking her, but she knew there was no turning back. From now on she would only look forward.

"Hey Greta, I just wanted to let you know I invited Shane to join us for dinner tonight. I hope you don't mind," Gabe told her a few weeks later.

"Not at all, Gabe. That's great!" she answered a little too enthusiastically. Greta hated the way her heart quickened knowing Shane would be there. She put down the phone and wondered, *What's wrong with me?* Since the holidays, they were often a threesome for dinner. And those were her favorite meals.

Her love for Gabe was beyond question, yet there was such a magnetic attraction to Shane. *Stop it, Greta!* She refused to be *that kind of woman.*

Greta checked her appearance in the full-length mirror, frowned, and walked into her closet. After several changes, she settled on the charcoal gray sweater that draped softly around her shoulders. Adding a pair of simple, silver drop earrings, she took a final look at her reflection. *Better...*

"It looks like Shane is already here. There's his car," Gabe said when they got to the restaurant. Greta's smile broadened as she saw him standing by the entrance.

They were seated immediately, ordered drinks and appetizers, and relaxed into easy conversation.

"Shane, tell Greta the story you told me about the anesthetist." Greta turned to Shane in anticipation. His hospital stories were always entertaining.

"Well, you have to know, Josef is a serious-minded young man... and extremely efficient. So I've come to depend on him to be on top of things. But not as on top of things as he was yesterday," he grinned. "He's one of the best nurses I work with... however, I think we found his Achilles heel."

Greta was hanging on every word but at the same time was aware of Gabe leaning back in his seat watching her. She sat back in her chair guiltily and deliberately tried to turn her attention to Gabe. But Gabe said, "Now get this..." and directed her attention back to his friend's story.

Shane described his anesthetist's encounter with a beautiful young redhead who obviously found him quite attractive. "Oh, did I mention, all the ladies seem to share that opinion? Anyway, I'm not sure what she said to him, but when he pulled back the curtain his face was about the color of these menus!"

Greta laughed looking at their burgundy color. Shane's eyes crinkled.

"He told me later that she said, 'You can sit by my bed anytime... or climb on in...'"

"Oh my God!" Greta's mouth dropped open. "Seriously?"

"Yep. Josef freaked and in his effort to get out of there stat, tripped, lost his balance and nearly fell on top of her. The last thing he heard as he escaped was, 'Oh Doctor!' He said he had no desire to go back and correct her mistake."

Greta and Gabe both laughed, imagining the young man's embarrassment, but it wasn't the story as much as Shane's charm that drew her in. She had nearly forgotten Gabe was there.

She smiled at Gabe, hoping he hadn't noticed yet fearing he had. He was looking back at her with an expression she didn't understand.

He doesn't look at all upset, she thought. But she knew he must be. Greta was puzzled and confused. She felt guilty yet didn't know why.

Shane went on talking, unaware of the unspoken exchange between his good friend and the beautiful woman.

When dinner was over, the three collected their coats and headed for the parking lot.

"Greta, I'm sorry, but I'm really tired," said Gabe. "Would you mind getting a ride home with Shane tonight? Or do you have to get back to the hospital?"

"No, I'm not on call tonight," Shane said quickly, "and I'd be happy to take you home, Greta. If that's okay with you?"

Greta looked from one to the other uneasily and asked, "Gabe, are you feeling all right? Are you sure you're okay to drive?"

"Stop, Greta," he laughed. "I'm fine! Stop being a mother hen and enjoy the rest of your evening."

Gabe winked as he opened his car door and hopped in. With a smile and wave, he backed out of his parking place, and Greta was left awkwardly standing by Shane.

"I hope you don't mind being stuck with me, Greta." The doctor's voice was barely above a whisper.

"Not at all," she smiled in guilty reply.

"Would you like to come in?" Greta asked hopefully. She felt like a teenager on her first date.

Shane followed Greta into the kitchen and took a seat at the counter. There was a comfortable silence while she made hot chocolate. Greta hummed happily and immersed herself in the task, warming milk over the stove and stirring the cocoa until all the lumps disappeared.

She turned and set two empty cups on the counter and looked up. "Oh!" she startled. She had expected to see Gabe sitting there. Heat rushed to her cheeks.

"What is it?" Shane asked curiously.

"I'm sorry," she answered too quickly, then added laughing, "I'm just so used to Gabe sitting there that I…"

Shane jumped in, "You know, it is peculiar. I mean, I know you and Gabe have been seeing each other for a few months, and spending a lot of time together, yet he's the one who's kind of setting us up." Shane hesitated and his brow wrinkled. "Greta, I don't mean to get too personal, but just how serious are you two? Are you, you know, a couple? Because if you are, I'll back off. I like Gabe. He's a good friend. I don't want to hurt him… or you."

"No, I know," Greta replied. "I would never do anything to hurt Gabe. He's helped me so much in the short time I've known him."

"Yeah, me too," said Shane.

Greta's eyebrows shot up. "We're not, you know, I mean we haven't...." she stammered. "We're not a couple the way you mean."

"So, that's what I thought. It was almost like he was telling me that you weren't off limits. That probably sounds awful, but I don't mean to offend you."

"No," she laughed a little. "I'm not offended." Releasing her breath, she added, "I'm really kind of relieved." Greta poured hot chocolate into the two mugs and handed him one. She led the way back to the living room. "I'm not really sure how to describe what it is that Gabe and I have. No, we're not intimate..." Her cheeks flushed red with the admission, "but I do love him." Greta looked down into her cup and smiled. Her head tilted as she struggled to express what she felt. "I mean I love him in a way I can't really put into words. It's not like I've ever felt about anyone else. It's hard to explain." Encouraged by the understanding she saw in Shane's eyes, she added, "I just know he's a very special person in my life. He's helped me in ways I can't even describe."

"I know, Greta."

She looked at him questioningly. "How?"

"Well, I don't know exactly how he's helped you, but I know what you mean because I feel the same way about him. He's changed me. He's changed the way I think and feel about things." Shane laughed with embarrassment. "I guess that sounds strange."

"No, it doesn't," she said. "Not at all. What is it?"

"There's something about Gabe, Greta. I can't quite put my finger on it, but he's not like anyone I've ever known." Greta nodded in agreement. Shane paused then lowered his head and added, "He's not well."

Greta's head jerked up. "He's sick? I knew it! What's wrong with him? Is it serious?" Panic chased out the questions she'd been holding back.

"Greta, listen to me. Calm down and just listen. I'm not just Gabe's friend. I'm his doctor, and I've already said too much."

"What do you mean? What's wrong with him, Shane? Tell me!"

"What I'm trying to tell you is I can't talk about what's wrong with him. It's doctor-patient confidentiality. I can't."

She looked at him imploringly. "Shane..." her voice cracked as the first tears slid down her cheek.

Shane pulled her into his arms. Greta hung onto the strength she felt in them.

Chapter 35

Don Taylor drove around for a while before going home. He hated the empty house. He never thought he'd miss his wife if she wasn't around, but the silence seemed to mock him, and now there was no one to blame for aggravating him.

Kim had been avoiding him since the last time they fought. He didn't remember that night too clearly, but he knew she had done something that really got under his skin. She had a habit of saying and doing things just to make him mad.

Women, he thought. *They just gotta needle ya 'til you can't stand it anymore. Then they wonder why you blow up!* Pulling up in front of the house, Taylor was surprised to see his wife's car parked in the driveway. *I hope she finally got some damn groceries. I oughta teach her a lesson for going off like that, not telling me where she was.*

He tried to open the front door, but it was locked. Angrily Don pulled his keys back out of his pocket.

"What the hell?" he shouted. The key didn't fit in the lock. Don pounded on the door with his fist. "Kim! Open this damn door!"

The door swung open, but it was not his wife standing on the other side. Bobby stood a full three inches taller than his father, and it was obvious he worked out.

"Bobby, what are you doing here? What's going on?" Don grumbled.

"I'll tell you what's going on, Dad. You're going to get your things and get out of here."

"What? The hell I am!" he said trying to push past his son.

He saw Kim standing in the middle of the living room. There was a large suitcase and a couple of boxes on the floor next to her.

"Oh, no you don't!" he yelled. "I'll be damned if you're going to throw me out of my own house." He puffed himself up and went for his wife, but Bobby stepped between them.

"I've got a piece of paper here that says differently, Dad. I think you'd better get yourself a lawyer. And don't forget," Bobby continued, "all Mom has to do is say the word, and your ass is in jail. I wouldn't push it if I were you." Bobby spoke calmly.

Don could see the resolve in his son's eyes. He was losing his position of power over the two of them. He didn't like it. He didn't like it one bit.

"Jail?" he laughed, "What? Just for coming into my own house?"

Kim, who hadn't said a word until now, spoke up. "No, Don, not for coming in the house. Bobby knows everything. He knows about what you did to Greta." She took a step forward to stand by her son's side. She didn't shy away from her husband's stare but looked straight into his eyes. "And he knows you could go to jail for it."

"You bitch..."

"That's enough, Dad," Bobby interrupted. "You need to go before this gets any uglier. I'm not going to let you hurt Mom anymore."

Don saw the look of angry determination on his son's face and grew even more furious with his wife.

Now she's turning my own son against me. Without another word, he grabbed the suitcase and headed for the door. No one spoke as he carried it out and threw it in the backseat of his car.

When he turned to go back in for the boxes, he saw the front door closing. Two flimsy cardboard boxes sat on the front porch. He heard the loud click of the deadbolt.

"Son of a bitch!" he yelled.

Don Taylor slammed the car in reverse, backed out, then screeched away from the house wondering where the hell he was supposed to go now.

Chapter 36

The next morning Greta awoke slowly. She had been dancing to the sounds of Chopin's *Nocturne in E-Flat Major*. She could still hear it and didn't want to let it go. But it was fading and with its passing was the growing anxiety about Gabe.

She came fully awake remembering Shane's words from the night before. Greta called in to let her secretary know she wouldn't be coming to the office today, assuring her that she was all right but needed to take some personal time to help a friend.

An hour later she was dressed and poised to go check up on Gabe. He'd agreed to meet her for an early lunch.

Greta spent the rest of the morning worrying, pacing, and drinking way too much coffee. "Maybe I should have gone to work. The waiting is killing me." Greta drained the dregs of her third cup and placed it in the sink.

Greta pulled into the parking lot fifteen minutes early. Relief flooded her system when she saw Gabe walking toward her.

When they were seated, Greta studied his face looking for any signs of illness.

"What is it, Greta? Why are you looking at me like that?"

"Sorry, I didn't mean to stare."

"Then how come you're still doing it?" Gabe laughed. Slowly his smile dissolved, and he reached across the table to put his hand over hers. "Okay, Greta, what's going on? Let's have it."

"What, what do you mean?" Greta held her breath and looked away. *Does he know about me and Shane?*

"I mean, why are looking at me like I have a wart on my nose?" he laughed. Gabe reached up and touched his nose in mock horror.

Letting out the breath she'd been holding, she explained cautiously. "Gabe, I'm sorry." She studied his face for any clues. "I'm worried about you."

"Well, that's nothing new. You've gotten to be my own personal little worrywart lately." He tried to laugh again but it fell short of the target. "Seriously, Greta, why the sudden need to see me? To check on me?"

Greta looked down at her plate searching for the right words. They weren't there.

"Oh, wait, you were with Shane last night. Did he say something to scare you? I guess maybe leaving the two of you together wasn't such a good idea after all." *Oh God, he does know.* Greta tried to read his face—to see if he was angry—*What if we were wrong?* But Gabe only looked curious—not angry.

"Gabe..."

The waiter interrupted to take their order. Greta asked for more time.

"Gabe, I..." Greta started.

"I think we'd better check the menu, don't you?" he interrupted.

Greta's mind raced. She stared at the menu without seeing. When the waiter came back, embarrassed, she ordered the first thing she saw. She felt Gabe watching her and finally broke the silence.

"To tell the truth, I did ask, but Shane wouldn't tell me anything." Greta hoped this was what he was actually talking about. "You know, doctor-patient confidentiality and all. But I could tell he's concerned about you."

As she spoke, Greta continued to examine Gabe's appearance. He had definitely lost more weight and his color was terrible.

"Gabe, can't you tell me what's wrong? And don't say 'nothing'! I'm not blind or stupid!"

He smiled wanly but didn't respond. After several moments, he spoke softly. "Okay, you deserve to know the truth. Yes, I am sick."

Greta gasped and reached for his hand. She saw sympathy in his eyes. He squeezed her hand. Through the blur of tears that suddenly filled her eyes, she could see he was the one now struggling for words.

"Greta, it's going to be all right. Please don't cry. It's okay."

"Did... did Shane say that you're getting better?" She remembered the concern in Shane's eyes the night before.

"Trust me, Greta. I'm not afraid, and I don't want you to be."

Gabe insisted on changing the subject, so Greta blinked back the tears, dried her sweaty palms on her napkin and tried to put her anxieties aside. But her mind continued to race. Finally she blurted out, "Gabe, tell me the truth. How sick are you?"

"My dear girl, I wouldn't dream of leaving you so soon. I need to know that you're going to be all right," he said looking into her eyes.

Greta felt slightly reassured until she realized, *But he didn't really answer the question.* Then another thought crept back into her mind. *What if he never meant for me to be with Shane?*

Again her eyes searched his face and her chest tightened. *Is Gabe going to die?*

Chapter 37

By the time they'd finished lunch and said goodbye, it was mid-afternoon. Greta wasn't in any mood to go back to the office. Instead, she took a walk around the harbor.

It was cold, and Greta hoped the cool air might clear her muddled mind. But as she walked along, she felt uneasy. She had the sense that someone was watching her...

Glancing back several times, Greta saw nothing. Yet the tiny hairs stood up on the back of her neck. She quickened her pace and escaped into a busy shop.

She moved down the aisles glancing at scarves and pocketbooks, but her eyes darted back to the entrance. She felt evil lurking.

Finally convinced she was being foolish, she crept toward the exit. Greta scanned the walkway before her hasty retreat to the car. *Stop it, Greta... get a grip!* With a quick glance in the rearview mirror, she eased into traffic and headed home.

From the shadows of the alleyway a figure slowly emerged as Greta's tail lights sped into the distance. Don Taylor sauntered back to the garage where he'd left his car. The sneer on his face reflected the malice of his intentions.

Chapter 38

After confronting Gabe about his illness, Greta felt no better, no more enlightened. He had been evasive, and she knew she should respect his wishes. That didn't make it any easier. She just had to know if he was going to be all right... and if her love for Shane was a betrayal. The very idea of hurting him crushed her. But she could no longer deny the love she felt for Shane.

One night in early February, Greta and Shane met for a light meal at Camden Pub down on Pratt Street.

"I called Gabe to see if he could join us, but it went straight to voicemail," Greta told Shane as they slid into their booth. "I told him where we'd be... haven't heard back though." She checked Shane's face for concern, but seeing none went on, "I hope he's okay." Gabe rarely joined them anymore.

"He's been working some pretty long hours lately, Greta. If he's not at the office, he might just be worn out from all the paperwork." Shane avoided her questioning gaze, and Greta knew it was useless. "Do you know what you want to eat?" he asked, changing the subject. She would get no new information on Gabe's health from Shane tonight.

Once they placed their order, Greta leaned back and looked across the table at the man she was with. She liked what she saw. She loved the set of his jaw and the way he smiled with his eyes. In that moment she thought only of Shane.

"Those guys are going to be toast by the end of the night," he said with a widening grin. Greta looked in the direction of his gaze and laughed. Seven young men were toasting and ribbing the eighth. It quickly became obvious it was a bachelor party. Greta and Shane enjoyed watching and joked about their antics while they ate.

But when they went back to the car the mood changed. Shane drove them home in relative silence.

As he pulled into her driveway and parked, Shane asked, "What is it? You're awfully quiet, and you look so sad. What's on your mind?"

"It's Gabe. Have you seen him or talked to him lately?"

"Not in a couple of weeks."

"I'm worried about him. He's been avoiding me, and I'm afraid he's gotten worse and just doesn't want me to know."

Shane looked at her, then still holding the steering wheel with both hands, stared off through the windshield. Finally, he turned back toward Greta. "Let's go inside and talk," he said.

Once inside they sat down together. Shane put his hand on Greta's cheek.

"Sweetheart, you know I'm Gabe's doctor, right?"

Greta nodded.

"And so I can't ethically tell you about his condition."

Again she nodded with her eyes still imploring.

"Okay, so I'm not telling you anything... but, well, I can't deny what you're saying." Greta's mouth went dry. Her chest tightened and she struggled to breathe. "Listen, I know you're worried. I understand, but..." he paused. "I have an idea." Shane took her hands. "How about if I find a way for us to meet with him so you can see for yourself?"

"Please, Shane. I need to know how he's doing. But how?"

"I'll think of something... but Greta," he paused, looked uncertain, then turned away before continuing, "I need to ask you something."

She waited expectantly..

"Are you in love with him?"

"What? No!" Greta flushed and searched for words. "I mean, well, yes..." He turned back to face her, but Greta saw a veil come over his expression and hastened to add, "...that is, I love him, but I'm not *in* love with him."

Shane sat down on the edge of the chair. Chin resting on his fist, he looked down at the floor. Greta couldn't see his face... didn't know what he was thinking.

"Shane, I can't explain exactly, but, well, he came into my life, and he touched me in a way that no one ever had before. I know that probably doesn't make sense, but it's just really hard to put into words." She sat down beside him and tenderly touched his arm. "My relationship with him is different than any other I've ever had." She added shyly, "It's not like what I feel for you."

Greta wondered if her words were pushing Shane away. Instantly she knew she didn't want them to. What she felt for Shane was a very different kind of love. When he looked back up at her, Greta stared into his eyes and felt a wave of relief.

"Greta, it's okay." He smiled slowly. "I actually think maybe I do understand. You see, I love him too." He laughed a little and added, "And *no*, I'm not gay," he said with a wink. "I think you can tell I like girls... well, one girl anyway."

Shane pulled Greta toward him and kissed her gently on the lips.

Greta felt a stirring, a warmth, familiar yet new. Her body tingled with excitement. She wasn't sure what to do, but she didn't pull away. When Shane's lips started to leave hers, she followed them, leaning into a kiss she didn't want to end. Their embrace grew stronger, and it was several minutes before he pulled back, still holding her tightly.

"Are you sure?"

"Yes." It was barely a whisper, and they were together again.

Later, lying in his arms, Greta looked at Shane with new eyes. She realized she'd never been in love before.

So this is what it feels like, she mused.

Shane opened his eyes, looked into hers and asked, "What are you smiling about, beautiful?"

"No one has ever called me that before."

"Really? That's hard to believe. You'll probably be hearing it a lot more from now on." And he pulled her closer.

The next morning Greta brought in the newspaper from the mailbox while Shane nursed his coffee.

"Shane, can we go see Gabe soon? I do care about him, and I'm so worried."

"Are you trying to make me jealous?" he teased.

She started to object when she saw the laughter in his eyes, then smacked him with the rolled up newspaper.

"Sorry, just kidding. Seriously, I know you're worried, and I had a thought. I'll talk to Gabe today and ask him to come over to my place for dinner. I'll tell him I have something I want to ask him about."

Greta wrinkled her brow. "Do you think he'll come?"

"Sure. Gabe's been like a big brother to me. He'll come if he thinks I need him. And I sort of do ... and you certainly do, too."

"So you don't think he'll get angry that we set him up?"

"I don't think so, Greta. Have you ever seen Gabe get angry?"

"Hmm, no... you're right. Gabe doesn't do anger." She smiled at the thought.

Shane was true to his word and Gabe accepted his invitation for Sunday. Greta spent the morning in Shane's kitchen making a big pot of stew. It was the perfect dish for a cold mid-Atlantic February meal. She put Shane to work helping with dinner preparations until the doorbell rang at exactly one o'clock.

When Shane ushered Gabe into the kitchen, he didn't seem terribly surprised by Greta's presence. She however was shocked. She had been looking forward to seeing him, but when she did, her jaw dropped. Greta didn't know what she'd expected, but it wasn't this.

"The missing man is found!" Shane joked to ease the tension. Greta held onto the counter trying to brace herself. "A nomad, he's wandered the desert eating naught but cornmeal and goat's milk." He threw his arm around his good friend who chuckled at the

British accent and wild story. He winked at Greta who had regained her composure.

"Well you must be awfully dry then, my good man," she said reaching for the wine bottle. "How 'bout a glass of something to quench your thirst now that you've found your way back?"

Gabe laughed harder at the charade until he started to cough. "Just water, please," he said trying to catch his breath. Greta grabbed a bottle out of the frig and quickly poured it for him. While he caught his breath she held hers.

She was sure Gabe had lost at least another ten to twenty pounds in the month since she had last seen him. His clothes were loose and baggy, his cheeks sunken, and his color was just terrible. *He looks awful!*

"Hey," Gabe said, "don't look so scared! It's not as bad as I look." He gave her that wink she'd seen before and been reassured by so often.

But it did nothing to reassure her now.

Nor did the look she saw on Shane's face. He tried to conceal it, but it was too late. She had seen the worry in his eyes... and if Shane—his doctor—was worried, Greta knew it must be serious.

"Gabe, are you all right? She looked from Gabe to Shane and back again waiting for a response from either of them. Nothing.

It was Gabe who finally broke the silence. "My sweet Greta. Please don't look at me like that. I'm going to be okay... really." With some effort he pushed himself up from the stool he'd taken and went to her. "Trust me, little one, everything's going to be fine." Wrapped in his arms, she could almost believe him. Almost.

He pulled back, holding her at arm's length, smiled and asked, "Now, how about that dinner you promised? It smells wonderful in here, and if that's beef stew that I smell, and fresh baked bread, they just might help fatten me up."

Again with the wink! she thought. "Sure." Greta made a feeble attempt at a smile. "Let's fatten you up."

Greta noticed that he moved his food around more than he actually ate but refrained from commenting. When they dug into their hot apple pie, Gabe looked at the two of them and asked, "So, is anybody going to tell me about what's going on here?"

Both Shane and Greta looked up. A split-second later, Shane guiltily turned away.

"What?" Greta asked.

Gabe laughed outright. "You two. It's written all over your faces. A man would have to be blind not to see the looks you two share... the... shall we call it... sexual tension?"

Now it was Greta's turn to look away with embarrassment. She was flustered and not quite sure what to say.

But Gabe was still smiling.

"Hey! Come on, what's with the shy bit? It looks to me like congratulations are in order. Two wonderful people have found each other... and I couldn't be happier for you." Greta gave Shane a sidelong glance and found his eyes smiling at her. "You guys are a perfect match, and I ought to know. It seems to me I'm the one that set you up to start with."

Greta turned her attention back to Gabe. "So it wasn't my imagination after all?" She smiled lovingly at Shane then looked at Gabe. The question in her eyes went unspoken.

What else are you up to, Gabe Engel?

Chapter 39

Greta was exhausted and agitated by all the traffic. She wondered why it always moved most slowly after work when she was already tired. A parade of red tail lights indicated an accident ahead. There would be no way out until she crept to the next exit.

In utter boredom she glanced around at other drivers and recognized the same looks of frustration on each face. A white Ford Taurus changed lanes. He'd been right behind her and had just cut someone off to get into the center lane.

Jerk! Greta thought. *Like that's gonna get you there so much faster.* Turning her attention back to the traffic in front of her, Greta inched forward, anxious to get to the exit ramp.

It was several minutes later, she noticed the motion of a turned head in the next car over. She felt someone's eyes boring into her. Unable to resist the pull, Greta looked to her left. The shock was palpable. His grim, unshaven face was all too familiar. It was the last person in the world she wanted to see... Don Taylor.

He was sitting in his white Taurus glaring at her.

Greta looked away, and forced herself not to look back. She felt trapped. There was no escape. As her lane began to move faster, she breathed in deeply, blew the air out through her mouth, tried to slow her racing heart. She had to increase the distance between them.

Seeing a break, she shot over to the right. Taylor was stuck in the far left of the four-lane highway. Greta ignored the guy behind her leaning on his horn. *Sorry, bud!* She heard more horns blowing and saw the Taurus change lanes. She wanted to push the cars in front of her forward before he could pull beside her. Every muscle in her body tensed with the effort.

Finally, the exit was visible ahead with flashing lights not far beyond. Traffic crawled as drivers worked their way over. "Oh great!" Greta groaned aloud. *Everyone's got the same idea!*

Coming to the exit ramp at last, Greta checked the rearview mirror. No sign of her stalker. She had lost him. She wiped her sweaty palms on her skirt and felt the pounding in her chest begin to slow. At last she let out a long slow breath. It was a few moments later that she took another peek. To her dismay, about three cars back, she saw a white Ford Taurus.

Okay, don't panic, Greta. she thought to herself. *He isn't the only person in Baltimore who drives that kind of car.* She changed lanes and then pulled into a convenience store.

Greta put the car in park and jerked around to see if it was him, but it was too late. The white car had made it through the green light and was well on its way. Taking a moment to catch her breath, Greta held onto the steering wheel to steady herself.

"He can't hurt me. He can't hurt me," she whispered, her eyes drilling a hole in the center of the dashboard. *If it even was him.* "He can't hurt me anymore."

She ran into the store, grabbed a bottle of water, then headed home… repeatedly checking her rearview mirror in spite of herself.

⁂

It wasn't a bad winter. Not too much snow, not too terribly cold, but winter it was, and Greta looked forward to its ending. By mid-March, the tease of daffodils was followed by an inevitable return to the same cold and discomfort. Yet hope was answered once more with the early spring flowers.

Like those spring flowers, the love between Shane and Greta was blossoming. Greta had moved cautiously. Those rather catastrophic past relationships sent up warning flares. *Don't move too fast. Don't smother him!* Yet she knew from that first night in

February that this was totally different... that Shane was totally different... and that what she felt for him was so much more than she had ever felt before.

And as the weather warmed, so did their love. They delighted in their time together. Shane spent most weekends at Greta's, and she tried to adjust to his strange schedule at the hospital.

His beeper would signal the need to go and care for a patient in intensive care, or the phone would ring in the middle of the night with an emergency requiring his immediate return to the hospital.

So when the phone rang after midnight, Greta simply groaned, opened one eye to kiss her sweetheart goodbye, rolled over, and then went back to sleep. It wasn't until early the next morning that she mistook the ringing phone for the alarm clock.

She saw it was 5:00 a.m., realized her mistake, and checked the caller ID. It was Shane. She answered, trying to push back the fear that suddenly gripped her heart.

Shane spoke calmly. "Good morning, love. Sorry to wake you, but I thought you'd want to know." She gripped the phone tighter, not wanting to hear what might follow. "We admitted Gabe last night." Greta jumped out of bed and began pacing. "He'd like to see you. Do you think you could take the morning off and come in?"

"I'll be right there, Shane."

"Whoa, slow down, babe. Just go ahead and get your shower, have breakfast, and come in when you're ready. You don't have to rush."

Greta sat back down on the side of the bed. "Are you sure? I mean, okay. Shane? Nevermind, I'll be there in a little while then." She hung up, sat paralyzed for several minutes, then shot into action.

Using all the restraint she could muster, Greta followed the doctor's orders. She showered, dressed, grabbed a quick bowl of cereal and coffee, and called to tell her secretary she wasn't coming in until at least lunchtime. Kathy said she'd check her schedule and take care of everything.

Greta poured more coffee in her travel mug, slipped into her jacket, and headed out to the car. On the drive over to the hospital, she imagined what she would find and wondered what she would say, but nothing prepared her for the reality.

"Greta," Shane warned, "he's very weak. You need to prepare yourself. He's really quite ill."

She gathered strength from the man she loved, turned and walked in to see Gabe. Shane was right.

When she first saw him lying there, Greta gasped and stopped in her tracks. An IV and oxygen tubing snaked around Gabe's thin pale arms. Monitors on both sides of his bed added to the scariness of the situation.

His eyes were closed so she didn't think he'd heard her come in, but then she saw him begin to smile.

"Hello, Greta. My sweet Greta." She rushed to his side. Taking care not to disturb his IV, she put a hand on his arm.

"Hi, how are you?" she said trying to sound cheerful.

"No sense trying to lie and tell you I'm fine and dandy, huh?" He opened his eyes and looked at her tenderly. "You know I was right, don't you?"

"Right about what?" she asked bewildered.

"I told you your dream was coming," he said softly.

Greta was confused. She couldn't remember him saying that, and yet there was a vague memory...

"Do you have any idea how much you've changed since I first met you?"

"I could say the same thing about you, Gabriel. You're skin and bones," Greta smiled. She fought back the tears that threatened.

"Seriously, Greta, you were like a frightened, lonely child when we met." His face grew more serious. His eyes penetrated hers. "Now I see you standing there, a strong confident woman. You have such a wonderful future ahead of you. I wish..." His eyes reflected a sudden sadness that vanished almost as quickly as it had appeared.

"What, Gabe? You wish what?"

"Nothing." He smiled again. "Whew, I'm sorry. I'm really tired. I just need to rest my eyes."

Greta listened to the beeps of the monitor, watched the pattern of his heartbeat. She couldn't walk away.

A slight motion drew her attention back to Gabe. His lips were moving and she leaned in. Ever so softly she heard him whisper, "No one can hurt you now."

Then he dropped off to sleep.

Greta thought fleetingly of the white Taurus then let it go. She stood silently at Gabe's bedside several minutes more. Tears filled her eyes as she watched him lying there so still. She didn't know Shane had returned to the room until he touched her arm. She looked up at him and said, "He's dying, isn't he?" Her voice quavered.

Shane could only nod and wrap her in his arms as his eyes brimmed with tears.

Chapter 40

Greta used a couple of vacation days leading up to the long Easter weekend. She and Shane took turns visiting Gabe at the hospital, but he slept most of the time. Whenever he woke and saw Greta there, he smiled and seemed comforted.

"How are you doing?" he asked when their eyes met.

"Me? I'm fine, silly. Shouldn't I be asking you that?" Greta said pushing his hair back off his forehead. "Do you want some water?" Gabe nodded, and she put the straw to his lips. He leaned back on the pillow, exhausted from the effort.

"Greta... you look tired." Gabe paused. "You're here all the time. You need to take care of yourself."

Greta could see that the conversation was taking a toll on him. "I'm not tired, and there's no place I'd rather be right now. Now hush up about it. Just rest." She saw the surrender on his face as he closed his eyes. *Don't leave me, Gabe,* she thought. *Not yet.*

Saturday night the dream returned.

The beautiful sounds of Chopin surrounded her as she and Gabe waltzed around the ballroom. As if floating on a cloud she looked into his beautiful eyes and felt their love like a balm.

The couple spun round and round, and she sensed his eyes upon her again. But when she looked up, she saw a different face. It took a moment before she recognized her father's eyes looking back at her, filled with love and peace and happiness.

"Daddy, you're okay now?" she asked.

He nodded, and then she watched as he danced and looked down at her, but it wasn't Greta. No, she was watching him dance with a beautiful girl… one who looked a lot like her. And then she knew. It was her mother.

Greta's mom looked so beautiful, so radiant. Her parents were dancing across the ballroom and looking back at her. They looked so very happy, so content. And Gabe was there, and he was watching her too. But there was a light around him. It was almost as though the light was emanating from his face.

And again Greta was dancing. Again she was looking up into two, beautiful blue eyes. She knew these eyes as well. These were the eyes of her love, and she and Shane were dancing, and the music was playing, and she heard Gabe's voice from far away, "Your dream has come."

☙❧

Greta awoke to find Shane sleeping peacefully by her side. It was Easter Sunday morning, and he wasn't on call so they would be able to attend church together. This was the most wonderful Mass of the year. There was nothing more stirring than the trumpeting of the message, *He is Risen!* The herald of trumpets rose as Greta's soul soared.

A few hours later, as they were leaving church, Shane checked his phone messages. With a look of concern he said, "I think we'd better go straight to the hospital." They had planned to visit Gabe after lunch, but the expression on Shane's face told Greta there was no time.

With a sense of dread they entered Gabe's room to see another doctor finish his examination. Shane asked for the chart, reviewed it, and moved to examine Gabe himself.

Greta stood by his side while he performed the cursory exam and feared she was about to say goodbye to one of the most important people in her life.

Without saying a word Shane put his hand on her shoulder then stepped aside so she could move closer.

Enveloped in the sadness of impending loss, Greta sat on the side of the bed and tenderly stroked Gabe's cheek. His eyes opened, and with great effort, he managed a smile.

She had to lean forward to hear what he said. "I'm not leaving you, child. You won't see me, but I'll always be there. I promise... You will see me in the truth of your dream."

"Gabe, I love you so much," she cried softly. "It's not fair!"

"You'll be okay." He glanced up at Shane, then back at her. "You and Shane... will take care of each other. You were meant to be."

Greta saw the effort it took for him to speak. "Shh, shh... don't tire yourself." But she felt his hand gently squeezing hers.

"It's okay, Greta," he smiled and added, "and it's time for me to go home." These final words were like a sigh, barely a whisper. Gabe was at peace as he smiled. She saw that familiar twinkle one last time. Then he closed his eyes and left them alone together.

Greta could no longer hold back her tears. The room became a blur as they ran down her cheeks. She turned and looked helplessly up at Shane.

He lifted her from the bedside and enfolded her in his arms. She saw her pain reflected in his eyes. He had also lost his best friend.

They held each other as the nurse and another doctor came in and turned off the monitors. *This can't be happening...* Shane finally guided her out of the room and down the hall to a waiting room where they could sit together in shared grief. The room was empty, and they sat in silence. Neither had words to express what they were feeling. None were necessary.

Greta grabbed some much needed tissues from a side table. This room saw many tears. The clock over the door ticked loudly. At a complete loss, Greta looked at the crucifix hanging on the wall. *Why, God?* There was no answer. There was only a terrible void. *How can he be gone?*

When Shane thought Greta would be okay, he went back to Gabe's room to take care of paperwork. In her overwhelming grief Greta had forgotten he was still Gabe's doctor. He would have to sign off on the medical chart.

She sat alone in her sorrow, now aware of the song running through her mind... "I'll be seeing you." Greta knew she would indeed see Gabe in the morning sun, but she knew she would also see him somewhere else.

Or at least a kind of reflection of him.

Yes, she would see Gabe inside Shane's eyes... And perhaps in her dreams?

Chapter 41

When they finally got back to Greta's on that emotional Easter Sunday, she and Shane sat side by side on the couch. They shared stories of Gabe, and then in sadness and loss, Greta learned more about Shane, the man she'd fallen in love with, than he'd ever shared before.

"I was going through an especially difficult time when I met Gabe last summer," he said. "We'd buried my father ten years before. But I'm embarrassed to say I didn't shed many tears at the time. I'd been carrying around a lot of anger and bitterness ever since. You see, my father was an alcoholic, and he was a mean drunk." Looking down at the floor Shane went on, "I grew up watching my mother suffer at his hands. He insulted her; he yelled at her; he smacked her around more than once."

Seeing how hard the telling was for him, Greta put her hand on his.

"I remember asking my Mom why he was so mean to her, but she usually made excuses for him. She told me, 'Your Dad works hard. His boss comes down hard on him, and then sometimes he has a few drinks because he's so stressed. It's the drinking that makes him that way, you know. When he's not drinking, he's not so mean.' But I knew better. When he was stone cold sober he was the same way," Shane added.

He moved from the couch and took the few steps to the bay window. Greta watched him silhouetted between the burgundy drapes as he went on with his story.

"I don't really remember ever hearing my father say a kind word to my mother," he said staring out the window. and he hardly spoke to me except when he needed something. I can't remember my father smiling at me or hugging me, or kissing me goodnight." Shane looked off into the distance as if vividly reliving the scene. Greta went to be by his side. She was momentarily distracted by a white Taurus pulling to the curb across the street. She was about to look closer when Shane turned to face her.

"There was this one night," Shane began again after clearing his throat. "I was fifteen. My father staggered in the front door drunk as usual, demanded his dinner, and after one taste, screamed at Mom because it was cold. When she reached for his plate to reheat it, he knocked it out of her hand, spilling food all over the dining room floor. Mom reached to clean up the mess, but he yelled, 'Leave it!' and backhanded her across the face."

Greta looked into Shane's eyes. She saw the pain there and all thoughts of the Taurus vanished with her concern.

"Well, something in me must have just snapped," he said. "I screamed at him to leave her alone. Then my father looked at me for the first time since he'd come in. The expression on his face scared me half to death, but I stood my ground. I remember what happened next. I remember it word for word.

" 'What did you say, boy?' my father asked incredulously. I gritted my teeth and answered, 'I said leave Mom alone. Don't you hit her again!'

"My father's face went from surprised to angry to a gruesome smirk. 'So all of a sudden you think you've got the balls to stop me, you little punk?' That's what he said to me." Shane shook his head. "Then before I knew what was happening, he was up out of his chair and coming across the room toward me fast. I took a step back but not fast enough. I felt the back of my father's hand connect with my jaw and I stumbled backward. Then I guess the taste of blood unleashed all the rage building up in me for years watching him beat and belittle my mother."

Greta remembered how her drunken uncle treated Aunt Kim.

"I charged at him. I can still hear his ugly laugh as he blocked my attack. I remember the nausea when he drilled his fist into my stomach, doubling me over."

Shane squeezed Greta's hand and went quiet as he remembered what happened next.

"Shane, I'm so sorry," Greta said softly. "Let's sit down." She led him back to the sofa. Either her words or moving to the couch seemed to break the trance he was in, and he continued his story.

"The worst of it was what he drove my mother to do." He looked up into Greta's eyes. "Mom wouldn't let him hurt me... I looked up and saw her running in from the kitchen. She was holding a butcher knife and raised it at my father's chest. He ran out the door. That was the last time I saw him alive."

"Oh my God... I'm so sorry Shane. I had no idea."

"I know. It's okay, sweetheart. I guess I should have told you sooner... but there's more. On the one-year anniversary of my father's death, Mom decided it was time for me to know the truth about why their marriage had turned so ugly... why she had nearly killed him, why he'd left that awful night and drove his car into the side of a brick liquor store.

"Mom told me he hadn't always been so angry. She said they were just out of high school and of limited means, but young and in love. They had hopes and dreams. They'd been married about six months when it all turned bad. Dad was at work and got a call from the police to come to the hospital. When he got there, a young detective told him what had happened to his new wife. He told Dad she had been attacked and raped."

Shane paused. Greta began to wonder if she should say something. She wanted to take away the hurt she saw on his face. When she cleared her throat to speak, Shane seemed to come back from where the memory had taken him.

"She said the guy was vicious and she must have looked pretty bad from the expression on my father's face when he saw her in the hospital bed. Mom said he looked at her then just turned and left," Shane said bitterly.

"After a couple of months passed, her physical wounds healed, but Dad was different. Mom said she struggled with guilt and blamed herself. She tried seeing a counselor a few times but couldn't get past it. She felt horrible all the time, not just mentally, but physically. She started getting sick every day. Greta, this was the part that was so hard for Mom to tell me. She was pregnant, pregnant with me." Greta took his hand in hers. "When she told my father, she said he was shocked. From then on, according to Mom, it was like there was a wall between them.

"So, I was born," Shane sighed then slowly smiled for a moment, "and Mom said she loved me the minute the nurses placed me in her arms. Once she held me she said it didn't matter who my father was. I was her son, and that was all that mattered." Shane's eyes brimmed with tears, and he brushed them away before going on. His smile faded.

"Unfortunately, Dad did care and he was hell bent on finding out if he was really my father. The tests proved without a doubt that I wasn't his. You see, Greta, I was actually the child of the monster who attacked my Mom and destroyed their marriage. My father spent the rest of his life trying to drown the truth with alcohol."

Greta wasn't sure she could hear much more. Her heart was breaking for him. *At least I knew my father,* she thought. *And he was a good man.*

"The police report indicated my dad may have fallen asleep or passed out at the wheel, but Mom never doubted for a minute that the demons he'd allowed to rule his life for so many years drove him into that wall." Shane put his arm around Greta, and she curled into his chest.

They sat silently for several moments. Greta thought he'd reached the end of his story, but then he went on.

"One night years later, I was sitting at home alone studying when Mom called. She asked me to come over and I knew by her voice that she was upset but she wouldn't say what was wrong over the phone. Of course I went right over, and I thought I was prepared for anything, but I was wrong."

Shane paused swallowing hard. Greta pulled her head back and looked up at him expectantly.

He looked back at her through a blur of tears and added, "That's when she told me she had an inoperable brain tumor. I tried to comfort her, Greta, but in the end she was the one comforting me."

Greta put her head back on his chest and held him tight.

After several minutes, he added, "It was just five weeks later that I stood by her bed saying goodbye. I couldn't believe she was gone." Greta felt her own tears on her cheeks but didn't move to wipe them away. "Being an only child of an only child, I didn't really have anyone to share my grief. I felt completely alone; I couldn't get past the guilt and anger. *Nothing* could fill the void. Nothing that is, until I met Gabe."

And now we've lost him, Greta thought.

"You're not alone now, Shane," she whispered. "I'm here." Shane hugged her closer to him. *Forever...*

Chapter 42

"Mmm, that's good coffee." Shane set his cup on the side table and smiled at Greta. She sat curled up on the other end of the big over-stuffed loveseat. Holding her mug in both hands she sipped, smiled, and nodded in agreement, relaxing with an odd mix of contentment and melancholy. They had both slept soundly and enjoyed a hearty breakfast. With little need for conversation, they shared a new unspoken closeness.

"Yes, good coffee and good company," she sighed. After several moments of comfortable silence, a thought occurred to her. "You know, I don't think you ever told me how you and Gabe met."

"I was doing rounds at the hospital last summer, and we literally ran into each other." He grinned at the memory. "I had my nose in the next patient's chart so I guess it was kind of my fault, but Gabe was lost. He said he was there to visit a friend in the orthopedic wing and must have gotten turned around. He had actually gotten off on the wrong floor. Anyhow, when we finished laughing and apologizing to each other for our clumsy collision, I redirected him."

Interesting... lost and on the wrong floor... Greta thought. She leaned forward expectantly.

"I guess that might have been the end of it," Shane stared out the window then a slow smile crept across his face, "except I ran into him again."

"Really? How did that happen?" Greta asked with growing curiosity.

"I was grabbing a quick dinner in the cafeteria, which was pretty crowded, and there he was. Sitting alone at a table. He motioned me over and said I was welcome to sit there if I didn't mind eating with a stranger."

"Seriously?" Greta's mouth had dropped open. *Coincidence?*

"Yes, why?"

"I met Gabe when he got lost looking for someone in my office building." She slowly slid her legs out from under her and planted her feet firmly on the floor.

"Really? That is a coincidence." He smiled.

"But that's not all. Later that day, at lunchtime, I ran into him again, and he asked if he could join me for lunch!"

It was Shane's turn to look surprised. "Well that's quite interesting..." As they compared notes, their individual experiences with Gabe seemed less and less likely to have been mere *coincidence.*

Greta closed the distance between them on the loveseat and Shane's arm automatically went around her.

"Well, I don't know about you, Greta, but Gabe came into my life at just the right time. I mean, I have lots of friends, but in truth, they could be more accurately described as acquaintances."

"Yeah, I know what you mean." Greta snuggled closer. "Other than Maria I didn't have anyone close either. And Maria's kind of busy with a husband and little one. So you and Gabe got to be really good friends then?"

"Absolutely. It seemed so easy and natural."

"Uh-huh," Greta knew exactly what he meant.

"We went sailing a couple of times, and before I knew it, I found myself talking to him about all kinds of things I'd never shared with anyone else." Shane felt Greta begin shaking with silent laughter. "What?"

"Oh, nothing really." She choked back the giggles she felt coming on. "I guess there's just something about sailing that loosens the tongue." Greta looked up at Shane's quizzical expression. "Nevermind, I'll tell ya later. So you were saying...?"

"Well, just that it was kind of therapeutic, you know?" he explained to Greta. "Losing him was harder than losing my own father... well, at least the man I *thought* was my father. Even though Gabe wasn't much older than me, in a way he was like the father I never had."

And like the father I lost, Greta thought.

"I mean, I could depend on him, you know? And he helped me understand a lot of things. Does that make any sense?" Shane laughed nervously.

Greta was amazed and took a moment before saying, "You have no idea how much."

༺๛༻

A few weeks later Shane made reservations for dinner at Rocco's Capriccio Restaurant. It was Greta's favorite, and she was thrilled. They arrived about 7:30, and had a feeling of déjà vu as they walked in. She warmly remembered the last time they'd had dinner there with Gabe.

Greta loved the panoramic view of the harbor, and she loved the man she was viewing it with. They ordered clams casino with their wine, Greta's veal scallopine was delectable as always. She even found room for a beautiful orange sorbet. Shane passed on dessert, but savored watching the love of his life enjoy hers.

They sat quietly watching the lights dancing on the water. Shane still seemed in no hurry to leave so they lingered over another cup of coffee.

Gazing out the window, Greta caught the reflection of Shane reaching into his pocket. She turned quickly and her eyes danced in delighted anticipation when he pulled out a small jeweler's box.

Greta gasped audibly and felt her eyes unexpectedly brim with tears.

"Hey," he said with the most beautiful smile she'd ever seen, "I think this is supposed to be a happy occasion."

She laughed and cried, throwing her hands up to her mouth as if in prayer. She bounced in her seat as Shane went on. She could feel the eyes of all the nearby diners watching them.

"Greta, you know I love you beyond anything I'd ever imagined. Never in my wildest dreams did I think I could feel this way about anybody."

Greta could hardly breathe. All conversation around them had ceased. She felt as though she was on a stage, in the spotlight... but all she could see was the man she loved getting down on one knee.

"I love you, Greta, and I think we both know we belong together."

Their waiter, who'd come to top off their coffee stopped in his tracks and waited expectantly. Greta's heart stopped as well.

"So I'm asking you, will you marry me and make me the happiest man on earth?" Greta wiped the tears from her cheeks. "Okay, now stop crying and please say yes."

Greta began to laugh and looked back into the beautiful blue eyes she'd come to love so much. She breathed her answer, "Yes, of course I'll marry you!"

Clapping erupted from the people at nearby tables. They were all delighted to have seen this special moment the two young lovers shared. A silver-haired man reached across the table and took his wife's hand, probably remembering a similar day in their life many years before. A young woman at another table looked hopefully at the man she was with.

Greta and Shane smiled somewhat shyly at the reaction, but then, lost in each other's eyes, soon forgot there was anyone else around.

Chapter 43

May brought warmer days and the relief of being outdoors. Greta could feel her senses awakening like the new birth all around her. She had listened to the weather forecast and looked forward to this weekend for days.

Sitting out on the patio savoring her coffee she waited for Shane to get home from the hospital. They were headed to Maria and Freddie's for the first cookout of the season. A 5:00 a.m. phone call had taken Shane off to the hospital, but he'd said he would be home in plenty of time for their afternoon barbeque. Life was feeling good... almost too good to be true.

Greta heard the car pull into the driveway. Shane was back early! She grabbed her cup and hurried inside. Glancing at the time she thought, *Geez, I'm not even dressed yet.* Then the doorbell rang.

Greta set her coffee on the counter and headed for the front door. *Maybe I won't get dressed for a while,* she smiled in anticipation.

"You haven't lost my house key already, have you?" she said as she released the deadbolt and opened the door.

Greta's eyes flew open and her jaw dropped. She felt hot and cold and clammy all at once. She had told him she never wanted to see him again, and there he was at her front door.

"No, you never gave *me* a key," he growled.

Greta hurried to close the door in his face, but Don Taylor pushed it open and came into the house without invitation. Her uncle had never been big on manners. Suddenly aware of what she was wearing, she stepped back and pulled her robe tightly around her. She fought the urge to run. To hide.

"What do you want?" Greta demanded. "I said everything I had to say to you when I saw you in December. Why are you here?"

"Yeah, you said plenty, but you didn't let me get a word in," Taylor replied bitterly. Greta was assailed by the familiar smell of alcohol on his breath as he spat the words.

"That's because I don't want to hear anything you have to say. You have nothing to say to me!"

"That's where you're wrong. I've got plenty to say, and you're gonna listen." His dirty, rumpled clothes looked like he'd slept in them. He took a step toward her but staggered to the side. Greta took a step back. *He's drunk!* The thought heightened her fear.

He pointed an accusatory finger at her chest and closed the gap between them. "I don't know just who in the hell you think you are, comin' into my house, yellin' at me with your high and mighty attitude, but you're nothin'." His speech was slurred.

"Get out of my house!" Greta said between clenched teeth. She turned to open the front door, but Taylor quickly stepped in front of her to block the way.

"No, Greta, not yet. I'm not done with you!"

Greta tasted bile rising in her throat. "All right, say what you have to say, and then you can leave."

"Listen, little girl, you owe me!"

Greta jumped back as he tried to poke her in the chest again with his filthy finger. "What?" she interrupted incredulously. "Owe you? Are you out of your mind?" She couldn't believe her ears.

"Yeah! You owe me! If it weren't for your aunt and I, what would have happened to you, huh? We took you in! We didn't have to do that, you know."

Greta could see his anger building and became a frightened little girl again. She wanted to run and hide from his tirade. "Please leave," she said hardly above a whisper. "My fiancé will be home in a few minutes." She added the last part hoping that it would scare him into going. She knew he wasn't nearly as tough with men as he was with women and children.

Taylor glanced nervously toward the front window but stood his ground. He had been practically shouting since he'd arrived but now lowered his voice. "I am going to leave," he paused, "but we're not done yet," he said menacingly.

Greta watched him slowly edge toward the door. Her mouth went dry. She could feel the heat rising from her neck as her cheeks flushed. She didn't know what to say. She stared in disbelief.

Don Taylor paused with his hand on the doorknob, looked back at her with a smirk, then opened it to leave. It wasn't until he was out the door and walking toward the car that Greta finally found her voice. She opened the storm door while staying inside with her hand safely ready to close it, and called after him, "We are done! Don't you ever come back here!"

Her uncle looked back just as she slammed and locked herself safely behind the front door.

She leaned against it, felt her heart pounding in her chest, and then allowed the tears to fall. Slowly she slid to the floor and buried her face in her hands.

※

Greta had no idea how much time had passed when she heard the car pull into the driveway. *He's back!* In panic she jumped up and leaned against the door. She scanned the room for something to defend herself.

Shane turned his key in the lock and pushed open the door. Greta collapsed into his arms.

"Greta, my God, what's wrong? What happened?"

She wanted to answer but couldn't get the words out between sobs.

"Are you okay? Shh, shh, you're scaring me. Breathe, sweetheart. What is it?"

"I'm okay," Greta finally managed.

"Okay, okay, let's sit down," he said trying to calm her. He brushed the hair back from her face and saw the fear in her eyes. "My God, Greta, what is it? Can you tell me what happened?"

When at last she found her voice, Greta responded, "He was here... Uncle Don... he just showed up, and pushed his way in..." the words came out in a rush.

"What? That son of a bitch! Are you all right? Did he... ?"

"No, no... he, he didn't *do* anything," she answered quickly. "But he was... he was here. In this room." Her face was contorted with pain.

"Greta, honey, it's okay. He can't hurt you anymore. I won't let him." He pulled her into his arms where she began to feel safe again.

Regaining control, Greta told him about her uncle's threats.

"Maybe we should call the police... ask about filing a restraining order or something."

Greta pulled away and looked out the window. There were no strange cars in sight. "No... I mean not right now. I just want to forget it ever happened." She turned back to face Shane.

"Okay, okay, we'll talk about it later. But listen, do you want to skip the cookout at the Garcia's this afternoon? If you're not feeling up to it, we can just stay here."

"No, no, don't be silly. I'm not going to let *him* ruin our day." Her voice quavered. "I'm fine," she said with more bravado than she felt. "But right now I just want you to hold me."

Maybe I should get a gun... or at least a baseball bat.

Greta's eyes told Shane that 'fine' was a bit of an exaggeration. He wrapped her tightly in his embrace and held her until she felt the tension leave her body.

Then they moved to the bedroom where Greta found another way to relieve tension with the man she loved.

☙❧

Sitting on Maria's deck sipping her iced tea, Greta felt like herself again. She and Shane loved spending time with their good friends and Freddie knew his way around the grill.

"Great steak, Freddie! I'm stuffed," Shane told his host. "Here's to good food and good friends." Four glasses clinked, followed by sighs of contentment.

Greta savored the smell of freshly mown grass and seeing the azaleas in full bloom. The serenity was interrupted by a little voice at the patio slider.

"Mama, I'm thirsty." Naptime was over.

Grinning, Maria slid the door open and gathered Ariana into her arms. Moments later everyone was in and out, clearing away the remains of their backyard feast. Almost everything had been taken in when Greta went out to grab her plate and utensils. As she turned to go back inside, she saw a shadowy figure move between the houses. She grasped the steak knife tightly in her right hand and froze.

Whoever it was disappeared from sight before she could be sure, yet Greta was certain she knew who was lurking there. Feeling a sudden chill she quickly joined the others inside, and, going to the front of the house looked out the window. She saw no one. But she heard a familiar voice.

"You'll be okay."

Chapter 44

Greta sat on the deck with her second cup of coffee and a stack of travel magazines. Leafing through one that featured islands in the Caribbean, her excitement built. She was totally lost in thoughts and plans for her upcoming wedding and honeymoon. Greta sighed with contentment as she pictured lying on the beach with her soon-to-be husband.

She was startled and jumped up when she heard the doorbell ring. *Who in the world?* She stopped short, remembering the last time she had an unexpected visitor. Barely breathing, she peeked out the window. She couldn't see the person's face but could tell it was a woman. *Okay, it's not him.* She looked up and down the street. The only car was the one pulled in the driveway. It wasn't a Ford. There was no one else in it.

Greta took a breath and opened the door enough to look out but kept one hand ready to slam it closed. "Yes? May I help you?"

The woman looked back at her with a timid smile. "Hi, Greta. It's me, Aunt Kim."

Startled, Greta finally looked—really looked—at her. "Oh my gosh, I didn't recognize you. Are...are you alone?" she stammered.

Kim Taylor glanced over her shoulder and looked back at Greta quizzically.

"Yes, it's just me."

"I'm sorry... come in, please." She opened the door wide and stepped back to let Kim inside then quickly shut and locked it.

Her mind raced, wondering what could possibly have brought her aunt to her door. Even more incredulously, why did she look so different? Yes, it was definitely Aunt Kim, but this wasn't the same woman she had last seen standing timidly in the Taylor doorway.

"Please, sit down." Greta indicated a spot on the sofa but took another look out the window before sitting herself.

Kim wore a beautiful red and orange silk blouse with a rich brown skirt and copper sandals—sandals that looked just like a pair Greta had seen at Nordstrom's. This was a far cry from Kim's usual bargain basement style.

The woman seemed much taller too, but it wasn't just the boots that gave her this new stature. It was something more. Her whole posture had transformed. Kim Taylor wasn't slouched over with her head down, drawn into herself the way Greta remembered her. No, she was standing tall, head held high, a woman of confidence and purpose.

"Greta, I hope it was okay for me to come."

Aunt Kim's voice called her attention back to the question. Why was she here?

Somewhat apologetically she continued, "I found your address when I was going through some of your uncle's papers. If you want me to leave, I'll understand," Kim was saying. Her aunt was still standing awkwardly looking at Greta uncertainly.

"No, no, I don't want you to leave. Please, please sit down. Would you like some coffee?"

Greta felt disconnected from this whole unfamiliar and completely unexpected scene. When her aunt declined the offer, she simply dropped into a chair and motioned for her Aunt Kim to sit across from her.

At a loss as to what to say to this new version of the weak victim she had grown up watching, Greta's mind jumped about, searching for the right questions. She was relieved when Aunt Kim took the lead.

"A lot has happened since the last time we saw each other... the day you came to the house." Kim looked Greta directly in the eyes for the first time. "I'm not with him anymore," she added raising her chin. Greta looked at her aunt wide eyed with disbelief.

"Really? Seriously?" Kim nodded. "What happened? I mean, I'm sorry, but..."

Kim interrupted, "No, don't be. I should have left him long ago..." she looked down at her hands, "but I was afraid." Staring at a spot on the floor, she seemed to withdraw back into herself for a moment. With a slight shake of her head, she went on. "I'm so sorry, Greta. It's bad enough that he hurt me, but I let him hurt you..."

Greta sat, speechless, waiting, seeing the line appear between her aunt's beautifully plucked brows. The next words were spoken so softly she barely heard them.

"It was true, wasn't it? All those things you said he did to you...? He really did that, didn't he?" Greta was stunned by the acknowledgment. Slowly Kim's eyes, brimming with tears, met Greta's. She quickly looked away, not needing an answer and said, "I should have seen it. I should have stopped it. I should have protected you."

Yes, you should have believed me.

But seeing her aunt's agonizing expression, Greta finally found her voice. "It's okay, Aunt Kim. It's over now." Unsure if it really was, she just wanted to take the pain from her aunt's eyes. "It's in the past."

"Can you ever forgive me?" Kim asked.

Greta nodded and reached over to take her hand. "We were both his victims, Aunt Kim."

"Well, not anymore!" Kim said emphatically. "He's hit me for the last time. I kicked him out!" Greta could hardly believe what she was hearing. "Bobby was there with me, and I had court papers to back me up so he didn't have much choice. You should have seen his face." The corners of her mouth turned up as she glanced back at her niece, and they both laughed nervously.

It was nearly two hours later when Shane found them sitting together chatting. Kim stood, and after a brief introduction, gave her niece a warm hug and said, "I'll see you Saturday, and... thank you."

As soon as the front door closed, Shane asked, "What in the world was that all about?"

Greta answered, "Something quite wonderful actually. You're never gonna believe it. I think at last I've met the real Kim Taylor.

Chapter 45

Greta put her last piece of jewelry, her grandmother's pearls, into her jewelry roll and placed it in her pink carry-on. Everything was ready for their flight. In the morning she would throw in her toiletries and be ready to go. She crawled into bed, turned the bedside lamp off, and listened to Shane's even breathing. He seemed to fall asleep the minute his head hit the pillow. Greta supposed that was an acquired skill based on his need to catch as much sleep as he could, whenever possible. A doctor never knows when he may have to answer a call for help.

Greta stared at the ceiling. *Geez, I'm way too wound to sleep,* she thought after tossing and turning for nearly half an hour. She slipped out of bed and tiptoed from the room. A smile danced across her lips as she realized there was no need to worry about waking Shane. She hoped a cup of chamomile tea might help her join him in peaceful slumber.

"Aunt Kim..." Greta was surprised to find her aunt sitting in the kitchen so late. "Can't you sleep either?"

"No, I'm sorry. Did I wake you?"

"Not at all... I haven't been able to sleep yet... too excited!"

Kim Taylor smiled lovingly at her niece.

Greta couldn't believe how close they'd become since the weekend her aunt had shown up at the door. She'd delighted in helping Greta with the wedding plans and now she was even going to be a part of it all.

"Well, Greta, I'm a wee bit nervous." Kim looked up sheepishly. "Did I mention I've never flown before?"

Greta carried her cup of tea to the table and sat down beside her aunt.

"No, I didn't realize that." Greta patted Kim's hand. "It's not so bad. I've only flown a few times myself, and the first time I was scared to death," she laughed. "I really was white-knuckled for the takeoff, but now I love it!"

It felt good... sitting there with her aunt. All those years living under the same roof... they had been strangers. Now they were family.

"Just wait 'til you're looking down at the clouds. It's amazing!" Greta squeezed Kim's hand. "And once Bobby meets us at the airport, you'll have him to hang onto."

"Yes, I'm sure you're right," Kim acknowledged lifting her chin and returning her niece's smile. She looked back down, staring into her empty glass.

Greta said goodnight and took several steps toward the hall, but suddenly felt compelled to look back. Kim was still staring into that empty glass. Greta saw a tear rolling down her cheek.

Setting her untouched tea on the counter, Greta spoke softly. "Are you sure you're okay, Auntie? It will be all right, I promise." She put her hand on Kim's shoulder.

"It's not that," Kim said hesitantly. "I'm just so glad you and Shane found each other." She got a tissue from the pocket in her robe and blew her nose. Turning to face Greta, she sobbed, "I can tell he's a good man, and it's time for you to finally have some happiness." She gently touched Greta's cheek and opened her mouth to say more. Then she closed it again and looked away.

"Aunt Kim, it's okay. Really, it's okay. You did the best you could. That's all any of us can do. Don't blame yourself." Greta put her arm around her aunt's shoulders. "You were hurt, we were all hurt, but you know what?" Wiping her tears away she added, "We're okay now. We're better than okay!" As she said it, she realized it was true.

Greta glanced behind her. She had felt more than heard Shane enter the kitchen. Her smile widened. "Speaking for myself, I would have to say I can't imagine being any happier than I am right now." She looked at her fiancé and added, "Well maybe a little happier in a couple of days."

Shane winked and Greta saw a little bit of Gabe in that moment. He kissed her forehead.

"I love you," he said sleepily, "I'm gonna go back to bed... just checking to make sure everything was okay. Night!"

Greta watched him leave. *It's really happening...*

Kim said goodnight and headed back to the guestroom. As she passed the bathroom, something caught her eye. It was the shadow box. She stopped and turned back to Greta who was following behind.

"Is something wrong?" Greta asked.

"No... no, but..." she bit her lower lip. "Greta, I wanted to ask you something, but... well, I'm not sure how you'll feel about it, and... and I'll understand if you don't want to," Kim hesitated.

"What is it?" Greta took a step toward her.

"Well, I'm certainly okay with you calling me Aunt Kim, or Auntie like we talked about... but, well..." Kim was wringing her hands and blew out a little breath. "I just wanted to say it would be okay with me... I mean I know you had a Mom... and your Gram was like a mother to you after she died... but I'd really like it if you would be comfortable enough to call me Mom."

Greta sucked in her breath and clutched her robe. She was stunned.

Kim laughed nervously. "Please don't be offended. I mean, I guess that sounds kind of crazy. I'm sorry."

"No, don't be sorry."

"It's just that you're like the daughter I never had. I want to be the 'mother' I should have been since you were ten."

Greta hesitated, not knowing what else to say at first. Then, with a lump in her throat, she wrapped her arms around her aunt. "I don't think you're crazy. That's actually the nicest thing you could have said. I'm... I'm not sure. I mean, can I think about it for a while... just because..."

"Of course," Aunt Kim jumped in. "Of course... It doesn't really matter what you call me. I just wanted you to know I love you as though you were my own daughter. I loved your Dad so much. We didn't see much of each other once I married," she glanced nervously away, "but I missed him. I still do," she said with a quiver in her voice. "You look a lot like your mother, but I see your father when I look at you too."

Greta whispered, "Thank you." Both women were laughing and crying as they embraced and said goodnight. Greta fairly floated back to her bedroom where Shane was waiting with a quizzical expression.

"What did she want? I heard you talking in the hall, but I'd guess it was nothing too bad from the smile on your face."

Greta crossed the short distance to the bed and climbed under the lavender comforter. "She told me I can call her Mom." Greta cuddled up against him. Mischievously she added, "And besides, I have a lot to smile about. In a couple of days *you* can call me *wife!*"

An untouched cup of chamomile sat on the kitchen counter as Greta slipped into a restful sleep.

Chapter 46

"Isn't it beautiful...?" Greta sighed as she looked out over the wild native flora. From where they sat in the little café, she could see part of the white sandy beach and the crystal clear water beyond. "I think we've found a little piece of paradise," she said as Shane took her hand.

"Eat up, Maria! I can't wait to hit the beach." Freddie took a big bite of his hotcake.

"Slow down, man!" Maria replied. "We've got all day." Everyone laughed. "It's not often we get away without Ariana. I'm gonna enjoy just takin' my time on this little vacation... and there's lots to do besides swim, yanno." A private look told her husband exactly what she meant. Freddie grinned and took another big bite.

Greta looked across the table where her aunt and cousin Bobby were sitting. "You're awfully quiet, Auntie." She wasn't yet comfortable with the idea of calling Kim 'Mom'. "How are you doing?"

Kim put down her cup. "Never better," she said with a slow lazy smile slowly lighting her face. "You couldn't have picked a more beautiful spot for your wedding. I'm just savoring the moment." She had not only survived the flight to Vieques, Puerto Rico, but had discovered that she loved flying. She put her hand on Bobby's arm and added, "I'm glad we could both be here."

Greta looked around the table and her eyes lingered on Shane. "We're glad you all could be here with us."

The wedding party spent much of the day enjoying the pristine beach and clear, warm water. It was so different from the crowd of people and umbrellas that lined the mid-Atlantic shores they were used to. After playing in the water, they collapsed onto their towels in delighted exhaustion.

"Greta, you'd better put on more sun-block," Kim warned. "It's okay to be a blushing bride, but you don't want to be a burnt one!"

"Good idea," she answered. It was nice having someone give her motherly advice. "Shane, will you get my back?"

"My pleasure," he murmured.

The application of lotion had never felt so good. His hands warmed her more than the sun ever could.

After a most pleasant seaside afternoon, Shane abruptly ended their leisure. "Hey guys, it's getting late. We'd better head up if we're going to meet Anita and the priest on time."

Greta had shared many emails and several phone calls with their wedding planner, Anita, and they were scheduled to meet with her at four o'clock.

"Okay, I'm willin', but it's gonna take one or two of you to hoist me up offa this beach," Maria said. Everyone erupted into laughter while Freddie and Bobby obliged.

No one took notice of the man sitting in the shade of a palm tree with a straw hat pulled down over his eyes. But he saw them.

꩜

"You said you would both be writing your own vows, yes?" Father Clavier smiled warmly as Greta and Shane nodded. "Wonderful! And who will be giving the bride away?"

"Well, actually, my parents are deceased, so we'll be skipping that part," Greta said shyly.

"Oh, I'm so sorry my dear, but that's not a problem at all." He took her gently by the shoulders with an understanding smile. "Times have changed and many old customs must change with them," he said.

The good father went over the order of things, then shook their hands, smiled and said he would see them at the wedding.

Shane looked down at Greta as the priest ambled off. "Are you okay, love? I mean, does it bother you that no one will be giving you away?"

"Not at all. Actually, someone already did... he just couldn't stay for the wedding." Her bittersweet smile told Shane exactly what she meant.

"Well, I'm sure not givin' her away!" Greta and Shane hadn't noticed Maria come up behind them. "I'm keepin' my Bestie... I'm not givin' her away... you'll just have to learn to share!"

Shane threw up his arms in surrender and Greta threw hers around her best friend.

"You've got a deal, Maria," Shane laughed. "Now we have a rehearsal dinner to get to, and I don't know about you, but I'm starving."

"Well, you know Maria," Freddie chimed in. "She's always ready to eat!"

"Hey!" Maria objected... but she also grabbed her bag and headed for the door.

☙❧

Greta fell asleep thinking about walking toward Shane in her wedding dress.

It had been a long time since she'd heard the Chopin melody, but on this night before her wedding she danced once more to the melody. She was waltzing again with Gabe, and felt the warm comfort of being in his arms. But as they circled the floor, things kept changing. She was dancing with Gabe, then she wasn't. Now she was happily floating around the ballroom in her father's arms, wearing her wedding gown, and her father looked so happy and content as he smiled down on her. He was talking to her softly, saying how she'd grown up to be such a beautiful woman.

"But of course you're beautiful. Your mother was beautiful so I should have known you would be too." Greta's father was beaming.

And then she realized she was no longer dancing. She was listening to the nocturne and watching her father dance with her... No, he was dancing with someone who looked a bit like her, but it wasn't her. Then she knew. It was her mother... and again the two of them looked across the room at her.

Greta could feel the love wrapping round her, a soft silky kind of love. And Gabe was there too. They were getting farther away... floating in light.

They weren't dancing anymore, or walking, yet they were moving... floating... away from her. She wanted to go after them, but she couldn't move. Panic stricken, she reached out but couldn't cross the distance between them. Then suddenly it was okay.

As they watched from a distance, she realized she wasn't alone. She was in Shane's arms. They began moving to the beautiful, familiar melody.

❧

Sitting on the beach, Don Taylor looked up at the beautiful hotel and watched one window after another go dark and imagined the couples behind them. He loathed the fact that he was out here alone while they were in there together. Taylor wasn't sure what to do, but he knew tomorrow was the time to do it.

Chapter 47

Greta woke early on the morning of her wedding. The sky was still dark with only a hint of the impending sunrise so she rolled over... tried to go back to sleep. *This is impossible!*

Not wanting to disturb Shane, she quietly slid out from under the covers and went to the window. The morning breeze caressed her skin and beckoned her outside. Greta tiptoed into the bathroom where she slipped into a top and a pair of shorts. She carried her flip-flops out to the hall and quietly closed the door behind her. The silence said she was the only one stirring at this hour.

Greta was happy... so happy and filled with anticipation that it frightened her. *What if something happens to ruin it?* A pattern of building her hopes only to have them come crashing down made her doubt the possibility of a happily-ever-after.

All right, Greta... you're being ridiculous! She didn't notice the young woman behind the desk as she crossed the small lobby.

"Is everything okay, Miss?"

"Oh," Greta jumped. "Yes, yes... I'm just going to watch the sunrise." The desk clerk smiled and wished her a good day.

Once outside, Greta felt the first butterflies and the cold fingers of fear gripping her heart. She pushed the feeling aside, refusing to let terror spoil her day.

At first she heard nothing... then slowly she became aware of the waves. The sound, the sweet smell... it was all delicious. She slid out of her flip-flops and let them swing from her fingers. The sand felt wonderful between her toes, and her anxiety eased with each step. At the water's edge, Greta turned to her left. She breathed deeply and let the warm water tickle her toes as she walked. Unsure how long she'd been walking and dreaming of finally marrying the love of her life, Greta decided to sit and rest and watch the night turn to morning. The sun crept up and kissed the horizon.

Entranced by its beauty, she didn't notice immediately that she was no longer alone on the beach. From the corner of her eye she saw movement. The hairs on the back of her neck stood up. She took a deep breath. *Calm down. You don't own the beach.* But she wasn't calm. It was a man. And she knew she was in trouble.

She knew that walk. *He can't be here!* He was coming from the direction of the hotel. Greta sat frozen... paralyzed with fear, she couldn't move... couldn't think what to do. To get back to the hotel, she would have to pass him. As he got closer, all doubt was removed. It was Don Taylor. *What is he doing here on this island?*

He was close enough now that she could see he was unshaven. His clothes were rumpled and his expression ugly. Panic finally broke her paralysis. Greta got to her feet and walked quickly toward the water. Taylor turned the same way. Greta stopped, changed direction back up the beach toward the walkway. Taylor did the same. *Why didn't I bring my phone with me?* She was trapped.

"What do you want?" she called across to him. "What are you doing here?" He kept coming. Greta looked around for help, but there was no one in sight. "Why can't you leave me alone?" she cried.

He suddenly seemed to cover the distance between them in one step and grabbed her by the wrist. Greta gasped and tried to pull away.

"C'mon, Greta... don't be that way. I just want to talk."

"I don't want to hear anything you have to say!"

"Well you're going to listen whether you like it or not," he snarled with a menacing look in his eyes. "You're coming with me."

"NO!" Greta tried to pull away, but his vice-like grip held fast. She wanted to scream but suddenly couldn't find her voice.

"You are not alone." She frantically looked around to see who spoke. No one was there. Taylor seemed not to have heard. *"You are not alone."* There it was again.

The stones and pieces of shell dug into Greta's feet as her uncle dragged her off the beach and into a parking lot. It was only then that she remembered she'd set her flip-flops down when she'd stopped to rest. Now she wished she hadn't left them.

One car was parked in the shade of a palm tree. They had moved in the direction of her hotel but were still too far away for anyone to hear her calls. Taylor opened the passenger door and shoved her inside.

"Get in," he said menacingly.

She wanted to run, to scream, to somehow get away, and yet she let him push her into the car. She sat there paralyzed with fear. He hurried around to the driver side, and even as she considered trying to escape, he was climbing back in. Taylor started the car and slowly pulled out of the parking lot without uttering a word. Greta's mouth was dry as she watched him out of the corner of her eye. She didn't understand how this could be happening, and she didn't know what to do.

❧

The sun was up. Shane scanned the beach.

"Do you see her?" Freddie asked.

"No, the beach is still pretty deserted... just a few guys fishing down there." His brow wrinkled. "Where could she be, Freddie?" Shane had been surprised when he woke alone. It wasn't until he had checked with Maria and Kim that his anxiety heightened. No one had seen Greta since they retired the night before.

In desperation he went to the lobby and checked with the desk clerk.

"Oh yes, Dr. Farrell," she smiled. "I saw her quite early. She said she was just going out to watch the sunrise. Isn't she back yet?"

After looking up and down the beach, Shane couldn't push down the fear any longer.

"Did you find her?" Maria, Bobby, and Kim came up behind them. "She's definitely nowhere inside the hotel." Maria laughed nervously, "What's she tryin' to do... scare us to death?"

The look on Shane's face told her if that was Greta's aim she had succeeded.

"I'm going to head down this way. Maybe she started walking and something happened. I mean, you know, like maybe she twisted her ankle or something." They all heard the fear in Shane's voice.

"I'll go with you," Freddie said. They decided Kim and Bobby should walk in the other direction, and Maria, whose pregnancy was pretty advanced, should stay at the hotel in case Greta returned.

It was Shane who saw them first. A pair of white flip-flops in the sand. He looked toward the water's edge and icy fingers gripped his heart.

❧

Taylor drove and drove. Greta's panic grew. *Where is he taking me?* He turned off the paved road onto a dirt one which narrowed to a single lane. It was full of ruts... obviously not used much... each bump and rut jolted her whole body and added to her fear. *Oh my God... he's crazy...*

Finally he stopped the car. Greta saw nothing but tall vegetation on either side of them.

"You betrayed me!" he spat. "I never said a word about the kind of girl you were, but you came to my house, and in front of my wife you said the most despicable things."

Greta's jaw dropped. She couldn't believe her ears. What was he saying? How could he possibly believe the things he was saying?

"I loved you, Greta, and you betrayed me. You had no right. I tried to show you how much I loved you, but you wouldn't listen. Now you will listen to me!"

They were far from the resort area now... far away from Shane. She began to realize how much danger she was in. She had no idea what he might be capable of doing. Gripped with fear, Greta wondered for the first time if he planned to kill her.

Near hysteria she began to cry. Taylor reached toward her and she pulled away, trying to duck from his reach and waiting to be struck.

But he didn't hit her. He began stroking her hair. Shocked, she looked at her aunt's husband in disbelief and horror.

His voice changed. "Greta, you know I love you. I've always loved you."

She couldn't believe this... she remembered that tone of voice from years ago... but suddenly she was sure of one thing. He would not hurt her again. And then she heard another voice.

"Greta, don't be afraid." It was the same voice she'd heard on the beach. *Gabe?* Now it all made sense. She knew her uncle couldn't hurt her anymore.

"Uncle Don," she spoke firmly, "You do *not* love me. If you loved me, you wouldn't force me to come with you against my will. You wouldn't try to frighten me."

"Listen, Greta, you don't understand. It's the only way I could get you to listen to me." His chin quivered. He started to cry, and she knew it was over.

"Okay, I'll give you two minutes. Say whatever it is you want to say."

"Sweetheart, you know I love you... remember? I've always loved you. Listen, we can go away. We can just leave, right now. We can go somewhere where nobody knows us. We can change our names, get married. We can be together forever."

Fear began to creep back up her spine. It was only now that Greta realized he was quite mad.

"Uncle Don," she said with more strength than she felt, "we're not going anywhere together except back to my hotel."

He started to object, but she went on.

"No, you're going to take me back, and I won't have you arrested for kidnapping me—on one condition. You will not contact me again. You won't call me, follow me, watch me, or in any way try to be in my life. You're not going to hurt Aunt Kim, and maybe you should get some help. Now, please drive." *No, he's crazy... not safe...* "No, get out, switch places with me. I'll drive."

He was still crying, head in his hands, and she knew he was broken. He would never hurt her again. With a new sense of calm, Greta drove back toward the hotel. The only sound in the car was the sniffling of the man she once thought of as her uncle and her tormentor. As she pulled into the parking lot, she saw the police car... and then she saw Shane.

Chapter 48

Greta, Maria, and Kim spent the afternoon getting ready for the wedding. The men of course were banned from the suite until the ceremony. Greta watched as Kim worked her magic on Maria's beautiful thick black locks. The final touch was the cream flower hair clip that perfectly matched her matron of honor dress.

"You look amazing, Maria!" Greta told her best friend. Maria smiled at her reflection, pleased with what she saw.

"Yeah, not bad for a fat lady! Thanks, Kim. I could never have gotten my mane to look this good."

"You're welcome... and you're not fat! You should have seen me when I was pregnant with Bobby." Kim rolled her eyes and they all laughed.

Maria stood and motioned for Greta to take her seat. "Your turn, girlfriend."

Greta sighed, smiled at Maria and her aunt, and sat down anxiously. Looking at Maria and Kim, she couldn't help but think how Taylor had nearly stolen this moment.

As if she'd read Greta's mind, Kim put her hand on her niece's shoulder. Their eyes met in the mirror and they shared a special look of understanding.

Kim had been furious when she'd found out what happened that morning, and shocked that Greta had let her uncle drive away. Yet she was the only one who seemed to understand why Greta hadn't pressed charges. "You have a generous spirit, Greta. I think you get that from your father," she had told her. "But one of these days that man is going to run out of second chances."

Greta's hair—once light brown, now enhanced to the color of the sandy beach below—flowed down to her shoulders, just the way Shane liked it. Kim slid the petite birdcage veil adorned with Swarovski rhinestones into her niece's hair then stood back to admire the bride. Maria and Kim's eyes filled with tears.

"No, don't do that!" Greta exclaimed. "You'll mess up your makeup, and worse, you'll make the bride cry and mess up hers!" With a concerted effort they blinked back the tears and laughed instead. Maria gently embraced her closest friend so as not to wrinkle her, then stepped back.

Kim looked at Greta and took her by the shoulders. "You are so beautiful, Greta," she said blinking back new tears.

"Thank you... I've never been happier... Mom."

A tear escaped Kim's eyes as she whispered, "Thank you, Greta..."

"Okay stop it, you two!" Maria thrust a tissue at each of them. "I'm not startin' this whole makeup routine all over again!"

They called down to the wedding planner, Anita, and confirmed that Shane, Freddie, and Bobby had already left for the wedding site before heading down themselves. As they crossed the lobby to the waiting car, they were met with approving smiles of several onlookers, but they didn't notice the one who followed them at a discreet distance.

※

Kim asked Greta if she had her vows.

"Yes, Maria has them. She's just going to hand them to me when the time comes."

Music was playing softly as Shane, Freddie, and Bobby stood with Father Clavier and watched the ladies approach.

Kim looked younger and more beautiful than she had in years. She was beaming as she came forward, took several steps to the left, and turned back to watch for Greta.

Freddie, standing next to Shane, beamed with love and pride as his lovely, pregnant wife, Maria, came next and took her place by Kim. He knew Maria's special smile was meant for him alone.

This is really happening... Greta's smile lit her whole face. She took a breath and the first step toward her new life. She heard the rustle of her gown joined by the shaking of her bouquet. Another deep breath. *The nightmare is over,* she thought, remembering her earlier abduction. *I'm getting married, Daddy... and I know you're watching.* She saw them all waiting for her... the most important people in her life, and then her eyes rested on her fiancé.

Shane watched, breathless, as he saw his bride walking toward him. Greta saw the way he looked at her and she had to force herself to walk slowly. She wanted to fly into his arms. They could have been the only two people on earth when their eyes met. Greta saw him through a blur of joyful tears.

As she approached the altar, Shane extended his arm, took her hand in his, and with a reassuring squeeze said all that needed to be said. Then, from somewhere deep inside, Greta heard a faint sound of a familiar melody. *Thank you, Gabe...* and then her complete attention turned to Father Clavier.

※

Don Taylor watched from the shadows in the back of the tiny chapel. It had been easy to slip in with everyone's attention focused on the bride. He stood swaying slightly.

Probably shouldn'a had that last beer, he thought. He tried to focus on what was happening and wished the priest would speak louder. He watched with a vile bitterness rising in his mouth. He slowly inched forward. *This ain't right,* he thought.

"No!" Taylor yelled fiercely. His voice echoed through the sanctuary.

※

All heads turned... shocked. Greta froze. She wanted to scream but stood immobilized until Shane pushed her behind him.

"It's him..." Greta breathed.

"Sir," the priest tried to speak.

"Shut-up!" Taylor screamed. "All of you just shup-up! So did my invitation get lost in the mail?" he smirked. He staggered forward two steps in Greta's direction, then stopped and stared at her. "What are you doing, Greta? You can't marry him! You belong to me."

Bobby took a step forward.

"Dad, stop it! What are you doing here?"

"Shut-up Bobby... Damn it! This is none of your business!" Taylor put his hand in his pocket and glared at his son who froze in his tracks. He had seen the damage his father could do and backed off. Taylor slowly turned his attention to the couple at the altar. "Greta, you need to come with me."

No, this can't be happening. Greta clutched Shane's arm. He muttered, "Don't worry... it's gonna be okay." Freddie and Maria watched in horror.

"Don," Kim spoke softly but firmly. "You can't do this." She moved toward her husband but stopped when he pulled the gun from his pocket. She looked back toward Greta, saw the fear written on her niece's face and eased closer to him. Bobby moved by his mother's side. Taylor's attention was focused on Greta—his obsession. But then he noticed how close Kim and Bobby had gotten.

"Get back!" he shouted. Taylor waved the gun around then saw movement out of the corner of his eye. He swung around and a shot rang out. Father Clavier fell backward. Greta gasped... she saw him aim the gun at Shane... then she saw something else. Her predator saw it too. His jaw dropped and his eyes went wide with terror.

Then everything seemed to happen at once. Kim grabbed her ex by the shirt front while Bobby wrestled the gun out of his father's hand. He stumbled forward and fell to his knees with a look of shock still on his face.

"I won't let you hurt her this time," Kim warned.

Then two local police officers rushed in and pulled Don Taylor to his feet. While Kim and Bobby filled them in on all that had happened, Greta tried to process what she had seen. As Don Taylor was being led out, Kim called after him. "You will never hurt her again!"

Greta was stunned and confused. "Did you see him, Shane?" She turned slowly and looked up into his face.

"Who?" He saw Greta's sense of bewilderment and wonder. Somehow he knew who she meant. "No. I saw Taylor look up at the altar, and when I turned there was some kind of light... and then everything got crazy."

They were interrupted when everyone gathered around in chaos.

"I'm okay," Father Clavier told them all. "I have to admit, the shot startled me so much, I guess that's why I jumped... just lost my balance and fell," he chuckled as he mopped the perspiration from his brow. Freddie helped him to his feet and said how lucky they were that the police showed up.

"After you got back and that maniac drove away," Kim explained looking at the bride, "I was still kinda nervous. So I asked the officers to be nearby tonight... just in case," she said breathlessly. "They were more than willing to oblige, considering the morning's events."

Everyone was speechless until Maria broke the silence. "Damn, girl!" As soon as she'd uttered the exclamation, she clapped her hand over her mouth and looked back at the priest. "I'm sorry, Father..." Her eyes were wide.

"Quite all right, my dear," he snickered. "Under the circumstances I think we can overlook a little slip." He winked and everyone began to relax.

"Now that the good officers have removed our interloper, I believe we have a wedding to perform." After some reassurance and a calming prayer by the priest, they were ready. Greta decided this wasn't the time, but she would tell Shane later—*Gabe had come to the wedding after all!*

A broken man wept in the back of a police car. But he was no longer their concern. A mere fifteen minutes after the police took him out in handcuffs, Greta and Shane resumed their places.

When it came time for their vows, Shane began. "I know we just met last fall, yet I feel like I've known you forever. It may be corny quoting something from a movie, but it seems so true..." He squeezed her hands. *"Greta, you complete me.* It's like I've been looking with no hope of ever finding you, but someone else found you for me." Shane's chin quivered and his eyes filled, "And he brought us together. I will be eternally grateful to him for that. Greta, I promise I will love you, support you, and be whatever you need me to be for as long as we both shall live."

Father Clavier told Greta it was her turn. She didn't ask for the paper on which she'd written her vows. She suddenly chose to speak from her heart.

"Shane, I love you like I've never loved anyone before. When I was asked who would give the bride away I said, 'No one.' But in truth there was someone. Like you said, Gabe brought us together. And I think Gabe gave the bride away, too." Greta's voice shook with emotion. "He gave me to you, and I will always be grateful to him for that."

Behind her, Maria sniffled and pulled out the tissue she'd hidden in her bodice.

"Dear Shane, I never thought I would find someone who would love me for who I am, but I did. You love me unconditionally, and you make my heart soar. I love you so much, and I love who I have become since you came into my life. I promise I will listen when you need someone to listen, I will laugh with you and cry with you, I will always be faithful to you, I will be there for you when you need me and I will share all that I am with you for as long as we both shall live."

Shane gently wiped the tear that slid down her cheek as he blinked his own away... and they laughed at themselves through the tears.

The priest's final words were like a song to Greta's ears.

"For as much as Shane and Greta have consented in holy wedlock, and have thereto confirmed the same by giving and receiving each one a ring; by the authority committed unto me, I now declare you husband and wife, according to the ordinance of God... in the name of the Father, and the Son, and the Holy Spirit, Amen."

Father Clavier gave the couple his final blessing then said, "You may kiss the bride."

He needn't have bothered.

They were way ahead of him...

Chapter 49

Hello, Mrs. Farrell. Greta smiled at her reflection. She looked at the fourth finger on her left hand almost in disbelief. *We're married... we're really married. Thank you, Lord!*

She pulled the brush through her hair one last time and looked at the result. The white peignoir flowed softly over her body, accenting every curve. Filled with anticipation, Greta took a breath and slowly opened the door. She gasped as she entered the bedroom.

"How long was I in there?" she asked in astonishment. Shane sat on the upholstered chair next to the bed which was now covered in rose petals. He was wearing the black silk pajama bottom she'd given him especially for this night.

"You like?" he asked with a devilish smile. She did. With a little help, he had transformed the room. A small table had been rolled in. On it was an ice bucket with a bottle of her favorite Moscato, two filled champagne glasses, and more rose petals. Everything was bathed in soft candlelight.

Shane slowly stood and lifting the glasses, handed one to his bride.

"Yes, I like very much," she finally answered. "How in the world did you do all this so fast?"

"I had a little help. Freddie was on stand-by," he said with a wink. "I wanted this night to be special." After just one sip, he took the glass from Greta's hand and set both on the table. He loosened the tie on her peignoir and slowly slid it off her shoulders.

"Mrs. Farrell..." Greta smiled loving the sound of her new name. "I love you so very much."

"And I love you," she whispered with a sigh. She put both hands on his chest loving the warmth of his skin.

Shane let his hands slide down her arms and pulled her toward their king-size bed. He slid the thin straps of her gown off her shoulders, and with the slightest wiggle Greta let it slide to the floor.

With a boldness she'd never felt before, Greta looked into his eyes and pushed the black satin down over her husband's hips. Shane stepped out of the pajamas, and in one quick move, scooped his new bride off her feet and dropped her gently onto the bed.

When he lowered himself onto her and their lips met, it was electric. There was no need for words.

Whether it was simply being somewhere other than their own bed or the enticement of her devilish husband, that night when they made love, it was as though for the first time.

Later, with the candles extinguished, they lay together in the quiet darkness. They spoke of the love they shared and the miracles that had led them to this moment. Don Taylor was nothing but a distant, ugly memory with no place in their new life together.

When they came together again, it was with tenderness. It was a giving love... with no thoughts of anyone but each other. Much later, with a smile of contentment dancing on her lips, Greta fell into a deep and peaceful sleep in her husband's arms.

It was sometime deep in the night when Greta's dream began.

She was at the beach with Shane walking hand and hand. It was amazing. The color of the water was such a beautiful blue-green next to the white sand which sparkled like diamonds. She could smell the sea and hear the sound of seagulls floating and soaring and diving. It was a magical afternoon. The sound of children's laughter and squeals of delight were all around them yet they walked in a peace and quiet that kept them apart from the friendly chaos.

She looked up at Shane who was smiling down on her knowingly. He nodded wordlessly toward the horizon. Greta looked and saw the most vibrant colors. They seemed to be coming closer, and then she was enveloped in the warm colors. They caressed her skin. She felt a tingling sensation, a wonderful tingling sensation that started at the top of her head and traveled down through her body. She was alone, but it was okay. She thought she should be looking for Shane, yet she knew she didn't have to. Everything was okay. No, everything was so much more than okay. It was beyond words; there were no words to describe what she was feeling.

In this moment of sweet sensation she was touched but could see no hand. Then she did see something as though in a mist from the sea. Out of the sea, it began to become more clear. Yes, she could see a pair of extraordinarily beautiful eyes filled with indescribable love.

Greta gasped with pleasure, unlike anything she'd ever felt before. Then she heard his voice. Gabe was asking her something, but she couldn't understand what it was.

"Gabe," she called out. "What is it Gabe? Where are you? I can't find you."

She was crying and running, lost in the mist, until she heard his voice again. "Remember, you'll never walk alone." Then her fear began to subside and the sound of the sea was replaced by a familiar melody.

She was dancing round and round the most beautiful room she'd ever seen. As she whirled around, she saw that the walls were an iridescent blue-green color sprinkled with a gold dusting. It was as though the sea had become the walls, and the sand was made of gold dust sprinkled over them. And she danced upon clouds, and above her was black except for the millions of diamond stars.

Greta finally looked up into the eyes of the man who carried her round and round the floor of clouds and saw that it was Shane, but when he spoke, it was with Gabe's voice.

"Don't be afraid. I know you can't see me, but it's all right. You know I am here, and I will be here for you, always."

Shane pulled her closer as they danced, and she knew it was Shane alone now. And then they pulled apart, and holding hands were spinning round and round. They started to laugh. But they weren't alone. There was another voice laughing with them, a tiny voice, and Greta realized the three of them were spinning around and laughing with unspeakable joy.

"Oh, sweet baby Gabriella," she sighed.

Made in the USA
Middletown, DE
09 April 2016